Forever Young

The Billionaires' Club: Book 5

AE Moran

The Invisible Publishing Company

The Billionaires' Club Series

Contents

Chapter 1: Dante

A sea of voices pours out of the grand hotel ballroom and through the lobby as I walk into The Billionaires' Club gala. This is our first gala of the year and it promises to be one of the best ever.

Everyone here is dressed up to the limit. The guys wear tuxes and the women were expensive designer gowns and tons of jewelry.

The billionaires in the room are all thriving and growing in ways I never could have imagined. Some are growing in ways none of us ever could have predicted. There are just as many women here as in years past, but this is different.

These women aren't just a bunch of random girls the billionaires picked up to be their dates for tonight. I don't see any professional escorts, either.

Some of these women are billionaires in their own right. Others are on their way to becoming billionaires. Melody Gottlieb stands over there on the arm of her billionaire husband, shipping tycoon Niko Holloway.

Quite a few of the other married women in this room are powerful business leaders who command the respect of everyone here, especially the billionaires. The more we learn about these women and the closer we get socially and personally, the more we respect them.

I walk over to another group where Lane Prince and his wife Samantha, Judah Hayes, and his wife Piper Legrange stand around with Derek Salazar and his wife Viviane. She's pregnant and I've never seen him happier.

I've never seen any of these men happier. Each one shines with a different kind of light cast over them by the glow of their domestic bliss.

Their happiness and grounded contentment shows in their work. The men work harder than ever and it pays off in spades.

Each of them is more successful than they've ever been—and yet all of this only makes them happier. They're so much happier now that they're married.

"You didn't bring a date, Dante," Viviane points out. "Are you trying to make a statement?"

"He is the statement," Lane replies. "He makes a statement just by getting out of bed in the morning. Are you kidding me?"

I laugh and wind up blushing. "It's a little more complicated than that, I'm afraid."

"What happened to Augustina or Paulina or Agrippina or whatever her name was?" Piper asks me. "That didn't last long."

"None of them lasts very long." I find myself scanning the ballroom. How did the subject suddenly turn to my love life?

"So what's next for you?" Judah asks. "You're one of the few unmarried men left in the club anymore."

"I don't think I want anything next," I tell him. "I'm taking myself off the market—especially for the kind of women who are interested in me."

"Aw!" Samantha chides. "You can't!"

"I can and I am." I smile at her. "I can do whatever I want. You can't stop me."

She laughs. "What kind of women are we talking about that are interested in you?" Lane asks. "You can't be talking about the usual gold-diggers. There has to be someone out there who is interested in you that you would be interested in her back."

"I'm not talking about them. The women who are really interested in me are all younger. Some are young enough to be my daughters. I'm getting too old for this shit."

"You aren't that old," Derek tells me. "How old are you, anyway?"

Viviane rests her hand on his jacket lapel. "Sweetheart! Don't you know it's rude to ask a lady her age?"

They all laugh and I laugh with them.

"It isn't really their age and I certainly never meet anyone my age that I'm interested in," I go on. "I don't understand it. I don't know. Maybe I'm just jaded because my last series of attempts ended in failure."

"I'm sure you'll find someone," Piper tells me. "You're the most eligible bachelor here."

I jolt and spin around to stare at her. "I am?"

"Of course. Look at you. You're gorgeous. You're one of the nicest guys we know. Who wouldn't want to date you? I would date you myself if I wasn't so much younger than you."

I look back and forth between her and Judah. She didn't say she would date me if she wasn't already married to one of the biggest, strongest, most intimidating men in the club.

He only smiles at me. He reads my mind. He has absolutely nothing to worry about where his wife is concerned. She worships the ground he walks on and it shows. No one knows better than he does exactly why she wouldn't date me.

I don't want to think about being the most eligible bachelor in the club. I don't want to think about dating at all.

Just then, Jackson Metcalf comes over to our group. He's single, too, thank Christ, and he didn't bring a date, either, so I'm not the only one.

Everyone can talk about him being the most eligible bachelor in the club for a change. He doesn't need a date. He really does make a statement just by getting out of bed in the morning.

I take a step back to let him join us. The others turn to greet him. Everyone loves Jackson.

The circle widens, but at that moment, one of the servers walks behind me and I accidentally step into her path and step on her foot.

She collides with me—or I collide with her—one or the other. It doesn't matter which it is because I bump into the tray of drinks she's carrying. My weight jolts the tray backward. It bumps into her chest and flies upward.

She corrects by tipping the tray toward herself—probably to save me from getting dirty. She winds up spilling the drinks all over her dress.

The servers all wear fancy clothes, too. The men wear tuxes and the women all wear long, black, sleek gowns. This woman wears a black, body-hugging dress down to her black high heels.

Shimmering sparkles wink and glisten in the fabric of her dress. This isn't strictly the uniform of black eveningwear the servers are supposed to wear, but it works and makes her look elegant. She fits right in.

I spin around and try to grab both the tray and the glasses falling all over the place, but it's too late. The drinks drench her dress. The glasses and all the ice cubes fall all over the floor.

"Oh, my God! I am so sorry!" I exclaim. "Are you okay?"

She stares at me in shock. Her mouth and her eyes hang open. She looks back and forth between me, her dress, and the mess all over the floor.

She's really pretty. Her long, copper-red hair drapes in tasteful waves over her shoulders and surrounds her petite face in a frame of glamor. Her hair sets off her brilliant green eyes with a spray of freckles across her nose and cheeks.

"I am so sorry!" she blurts out. "I didn't see you! I...I don't know what I was thinking! I am so sorry! I'll pay for it.....I swear...."

"It was my fault. No one is going to make you pay for anything." I hold out my hands. "Let me help you....."

I don't know how to help her without touching her body and I don't want to do that. She stands there holding the empty tray.

I bend down and start picking up the fallen glasses and ice cubes. She does the same thing. I put the glasses back on the tray and scoop the ice cubes into the glasses. So does she.

"I'm so sorry!" she goes on. "I didn't mean to. I didn't realize you were moving back. I was looking at something across the room. I can't believe I did something so clumsy. I don't know how to apologize enough."

"You don't have to apologize at all. It was all my fault. I stepped on your foot. That was my fault. I should have been more careful."

Her eyes dart around the room like she's worried someone is going to fire her or something. That's when a bunch of other servers show up with mops, rags, and dustpans to sweep up the extra ice cubes.

The server who spilled all of this vanishes into the crowd. I don't see where she went.

The others start mopping the floor. Some of them even apologize to me. "I'm so sorry for the disturbance, Mr. Helme," a guy in a tux tells me. His name is Ross. He's the catering manager. "Please go on with your evening. I'll handle this."

"Don't do anything to her," I insist. "It was my fault. Don't reprimand or even criticize her. She did nothing wrong."

He barely compresses his lips, but I can see he doesn't believe me. "I appreciate you saying so. I'll take care of it. I apologize again for the disturbance."

All the other servers evaporate into the woodwork. They take their mops and trays out of sight. Conversation restarts and the same throb of voices washes over the room.

"Are you okay, Dante?" Viviane asks me. "That was unlucky."

"I'm fine." I frown down at my hands. They're still wet from touching the ice cubes. "She got it worse than I did."

The others go back to talking about something else. I can't pay attention to them. I say a quick, "Would you please excuse me?" and walk away toward the back room. That's where the caterers and servers do all their work.

I hardly ever come in here unless I'm on the committee organizing one of these events. The whole point of the gala is so the billionaire club members can socialize with each other without having to worry about all the arrangements.

We're supposed to pay attention to each other and pretend the catering and service people don't exist—but they do. They're all normal people doing a job.

I walk into the catering kitchen and look around. The servers go back and forth between the service window, another drinks counter to one side, and back out onto the ballroom floor.

The servers come in with empty trays or trays loaded with empty glasses and dishes. The servers drop off all their dirty dishes at the sink and reload with either drinks or food to take back out to the gala attendees.

One of the regular servers comes over to me. "Can I help you with anything, Mr. Helme?"

"Where's the server who just spilled drinks all over herself? Is she still here?"

"Yes, Sir. She's in the bathroom getting cleaned up. I think she might be trying to change her clothes." He makes a face. "Ross is over there waiting for her."

"Thanks." I walk off in one direction and he leaves going the other way.

I find the bathrooms. The women's door is shut. Ross paces back and forth in front of the door with my hands on my hips.

He freezes when he sees me. "I told you I would handle it."

"And I told you not to get her into trouble because of what happened. What are you going to do—give her the axe right now because of one simple accident?"

"You don't understand, Mr. Helme. We've had nothing but problems with Emberlynn since she started working for us....."

"What problems? Is it because she's clumsy? Does she have accidents all the time?"

"No, it isn't that."

"Is she chronically late or lazy? I find that hard to believe. She was working hard right up until this happened."

"No, she's fine."

"Then what exactly is the problem."

"She's.....I don't know how to describe it. She's just...."

I wait for him to say something. "She's what?"

"I don't know, okay?!" he blurts out. "I can't describe it. She just doesn't fit in."

I raise my eyebrows at him. "So let me get this straight. You can't pinpoint anything about her job performance that's substandard or inadequate. You can't point to her attitude or her work ethic or her punctuality or her appearance or her behavior—and you want to take one accident as an excuse to fire her because you don't like her? Is that it?"

"You don't understand, Mr. Helme...."

"You're right. I don't understand because you haven't given me one valid reason to fire her. She could sue you for wrongful termination. Do you realize that? What you're doing is illegal—or you're planning to do something illegal." I make up my mind and raise my hand. "You know what? We aren't having this conversation. If you do anything to her—if you even look at her wrong—you won't be contracted by the club to cater these events anymore. Is that clear? We won't do business with someone who uses his influence to hurt his employees like this."

He opens his mouth to argue. "But Mr. Helme....."

"Walk away, Ross," I snap. "Walk away right now and don't let me find out you did anything to Emberlynn—ever. Is that clear?"

He shuts his mouth and hustles away into the kitchen. I catch a bunch of the servers, chefs, dishwashers, and preppers watching and listening to our conversation. Good. I hope they all heard me.

Chapter 2: Emberlynn

I pull a bunch of paper towels out of the bathroom handwashing dispenser and pat the water and alcohol out of my dress. I gasp in exasperation when I pull out the last paper towels.

My dress is still soaked and the liquid even saturates my bra. Now I have to work in wet clothes for the rest of the evening.

I'll just have to bite the bullet. I need this job to pay the rent and keep myself alive.

I dread walking out of this room and facing Ross—not to mention all the billionaires out on the ballroom floor. This is the most humiliating experience of my life.

I don't know why Ross dislikes me so much. I never did anything to him. I've already been hiding in here for too long already. I don't want to give him any more excuse to come down on me.

I pull open the bathroom door and freeze when I come face to face with Dante Helme standing out in the hall. He leans against the wall opposite the bathroom. It couldn't be more obvious that he's the one waiting for me to come out. I don't see Ross anywhere.

His head shoots up when I open the door. His blue eyes go hard and he looks down at my dress before he comes back to making eye contact with me.

He's the oldest member of The Billionaires' Club. I don't even know how old he is, but he's one of those men who just keeps getting better looking with age.

He's tall and he obviously works out—a lot. He's one of the best-built men in the club except for maybe Jackson Metcalf.

Dante fills out a suit very nicely and he keeps his short, grey hair combed to a point in front of his chiseled, weathered face.

"Are you okay?" he asks. "I mean....you didn't get hurt or anything, did you?"

"I'm fine, Mr. Helme." I walk past him and head back out to the kitchen. "You don't have to worry about me. It was nothing. I'm sorry I inconvenienced you. You can go back to the gala. I have to get back to work."

He only follows me. "Your dress is still wet. Let me replace it. You can't go back to work in wet clothes. That's ridiculous."

"I appreciate the offer, Mr. Helm, but you can't replace it now," I reply over my shoulder. "It's almost ten o'clock at night and I still have to get through the rest of the gala."

I pick up my serving tray from the drinks bar and stand there waiting for the bartender to load up the tray.

Dante stands next to me talking away. "I wasn't saying I would go out and buy another of the same kind of dress. We have extra clothes in the back room in case something like this happens to one of the members' dates or wives or whatever. I can give you another dress to wear. Come on, Emberlynn. Let me make it up to you."

"You have nothing to make up to me, Mr. Helme," I tell him. "I'm really sorry it happened. Please just go enjoy the gala and don't worry about me. I'll be fine."

"I can't enjoy the gala if I'm worrying about you. Come on. Just come with me and change into some dry clothes. I'm not going to be able to leave this alone until you come. Come on. I feel terrible that I stepped on your foot and got you in trouble and everything. Let me do something."

I finally turn around and face him. He's an incredibly nice guy. Everyone on the catering and serving team knows him.

He's usually involved in organizing and planning these events for the club. He negotiates with Ross and often interacts with the servers before and during the event.

He's always nice to the servers and he always compliments us on what a great job we're doing. He treats us a hell of a lot better than Ross does.

I take a deep breath. I shouldn't let Dante make a fuss over me. The serving staff is supposed to make sure the members, attendees, and their guests have a nice time at the gala, not the other way around.

That's just the kind of guy he is. He has a reputation for being an outstanding businessman and one of the nicest people in all of New York. You wouldn't think a billionaire could be as nice as he is, but he just keeps proving it every time he opens his mouth.

"I really appreciate you sticking up for me just now," I tell him. "I heard what you said to Ross. I'm grateful."

"Why does he dislike you so much? There must be a reason."

"I don't know. He liked me just fine when I first started. Then it all went south."

"Something must have happened. Are you sure you don't know what it is?"

I shrug. "One time he saw me laughing and joking around with some of the other employees a few minutes before the event started. He started glaring at me and it all went downhill from there. I think he might have gotten the idea that I was goofing around and not taking the job seriously—or something like that. I don't know."

The bartender finishes filling the drinks on my tray and I pick it up to leave.

Dante lays his arm across mine to stop me. "Just come with me and let me give you a dry dress. That's all I ask. I'm not asking for a lifetime commitment, Emberlynn. Just let me do one thing for you. Then you never have to look at me again. I swear it."

I sigh. "Fine. If you insist."

"I do." He takes my hands off the tray. I try to pretend that he isn't touching me like this.

His hands are warm and strong—much stronger than a man his age has a right to be. He even has calluses on his palms—probably from lifting weights. Anyone can see how ripped he is just by looking at the way he wears his suit.

He leads me out of the kitchen, down the hall, and back into the ballroom. I don't want to show my face out there, but no one notices me.

He actually puts his arm behind my back to escort me like we're on a date or something. He didn't bring a date to the gala. How is he even still single? Every girl I know thinks he's one of the hottest men in the club.

I see us walking next to each other on our way across the ballroom. We actually look like we're on a date. I look like I could be dressed up to be his plus-one for this event.

I'm not on a date with Dante Helme. That's absurd. He's one of the richest men in New York City. I'm just a server with a catering company.

He leads me down another hall and we leave all the noise and conversation behind. It fades into silence behind us. I can pretend that Ross isn't back there simmering with resentment over Dante defending me.

I don't trust Ross not to do something to retaliate, but that's a matter for another day.

Dante opens another door down the hall and leads me into a large room packed from wall to wall with clothes racks. Half the racks hold men's suits and tuxes in different sizes.

Women's ballgowns and sleek, designer dresses fill the other half of the room. Dante shows me inside and shuts the door behind us. "You can take your pick. I don't know if you'll be able to find anything that comes close to that one, but at least you'll have something dry to wear."

I go over to the women's side of the room. The dresses are all arranged by color. I stop in front of the black section and start flipping through the hangers.

The dresses are all different sizes, too. Some are miles too big for me and some are way too small. I finally settle on another close-fitting, body-con black dress. This one is shorter. The hem falls just below the knee.

"Will Ross give you a hard time about it not being long enough?" Dante asks.

I flip the rest of the hangers. "I don't see anything floor-length that will fit me. Maybe I should just keep wearing the dress I already have on."

"He won't bother you for wearing that. He won't bother you at all."

I make a face at him. "You don't know him very well, do you? He'll find a way."

"Then you'll tell me and I'll put the fear of God into him."

I find myself laughing. "Maybe I should just find a different job. I shouldn't keep working in such a hostile environment."

"Why do you work for him at all if he dislikes you so much?"

"I have to pay the bills while I look for something else. I've been looking for ages, but it never works out that way. I guess working for him is easy. It's a paycheck for now."

"What would you like to do instead? Are you trained for anything?"

"I worked as an executive assistant to Marianne Talbot for seven years before she passed away. That's when I started looking for another job."

His eyes fall out of their sockets. "Really?! Wow! That's incredible."

"It was. She was a great boss." I turn back to look at the dress in my hands. "I should probably change."

"I'll just leave the room. You can change in here."

He lets himself out and shuts the door behind him. I'm all alone in here now.

Chapter 3: Emberlynn

I shimmy out of my dress and pull on the new one. My bra is still wet, but it isn't as bad as I thought.

I put on the new dress, straighten it around my body, and run my hands down my sides and hips. The dress fits perfectly and walking around in something dry is a lot more comfortable.

I ball up my old dress. I might have to get it dry-cleaned and I don't have the money for that. I might even have to replace it.

I won't need to replace it if I quit this job. I can get another server job anywhere—and I sure as hell won't get a good recommendation from Ross.

I walk out of the room to find Dante waiting for me. He never leaves me alone. "How does that feel?" he asks.

"Much better. Thank you. I'm sorry I took you away from the gala."

He waves at nothing. "We have them all the time and it isn't like I don't see these people on a regular basis anyway. This is more impor-tant." He falls in next to me on our way back to the ballroom. "I'm really sorry it happened."

"If it wasn't my fault, then it wasn't your fault. It was no one's fault. It was an accident."

We stop at the threshold between the door and the ballroom. Most of the attendees and their guests are already leaving.

The servers are all back in the kitchen packing up for the night, clocking out, and telling each other they'll see each other next time—whenever Ross calls us for our next job.

"I guess we're done for the night," I remark. "I might as well go home and give Ross a chance to cool off."

"Let me give you a ride," Dante tells me. "Do you have a car—or another ride?"

I smile up at him. "That's really nice of you, but I couldn't impose on you any more than I already have. Thank you for the dress. I'll return it to the club. I promise."

"Keep it," he tells me. "God knows we have enough of them. You might need it for your next event." I open my mouth to protest, but he cuts me off. "Come on. Let me give you a ride home. I made you miss all that work. Let me make it up to you."

He doesn't give me a chance to argue. He takes hold of my arm and leads me across the ballroom. He says good night to a few people and we cross the hotel lobby.

He stops inside the big revolving glass doors to send a text on his phone before we go out to the curb. We barely get there before a big, sleek black limo comes to pick us up.

He opens the door for me to get into the back seat. "This is the first time I've ever ridden in a limo," I tell him when he sits down next to me.

"It isn't that big a deal. It isn't that different from taking a cab except that this is more comfortable."

"It's definitely different." I look at the little drinks fridge next to the seat and all the climate controls on the door handle. The glass window between us and the driver stands open so we can see him, the driver's compartment, and the street beyond the windshield.

"I might know someone in the club who is looking for an assistant," Dante tells me after a few minutes. "I can drop your name. You might get lucky."

"I appreciate that."

The driver interrupts. "Where are we going, Mr. Helme?"

I give the driver my address. The silence that follows becomes unbearable.

I wish Dante wasn't paying so much attention to me. Now I really feel bad. It isn't like me spilling drinks on my dress is any big deal. He's treating me like I got injured or something.

"I meant what I said," he goes on. "I want to hear if you have any problem with Ross."

I smile at him. "That's really nice of you. Thank you."

"Tell me if you quit working for him," he insists. "I might get the wrong idea if you aren't there at our next event. Tell me if you get an offer or if you decide to just move on."

I look up at him planning to thank him again. He turns to look down at me at the same time—and something changes between us in that moment.

I don't know what it is because our conversation has been so casual and businesslike until now. Maybe it's all the times he's been looking at my body, my clothes, and the way he's been touching me.

I realize in that moment that he isn't look at me like he's concerned about what happened. He didn't have to do all of that because he tripped over me and made me spill drinks all over myself.

He didn't have to give me a ride home. He isn't doing that to be nice—or not just to be nice.

He's so magnetically attractive. His eyes communicate so much hidden meaning without saying a word. He looks back at me like he finds me attractive, too, even though I must be thirty years younger than he is.

His age doesn't make him any less attractive to me. Why would my age make me any less attractive to him? It obviously doesn't.

I don't know what makes it happen, but he leans forward and starts kissing me. His lips send an electric charge through me and I kiss him back. I shouldn't be doing this with him in the back of a limo, but it looks like we are doing it.

His hands materialize on my hips, sides, breasts, cheeks, and neck like he's been aching to touch me all this time. Was he really thinking about this when he looked down at my dress? He never let on.

I don't think he was thinking about it then. He just treated it like any other normal incident. It could have happened to anyone and he would have dealt with it the same way.

He slides his hands up my sides, compresses my bra through my dress, and makes me whimper into his mouth. His other hand cradles the side of my neck and cheek. His masterful touch makes me melt. He knows exactly how to handle me to light me on fire.

I can't stop kissing him. He's hands down the hottest, most appealing guy I've ever kissed. I really want him to find me as attractive as I find him.

He slips his other hand behind my back, down to my hips, and pulls me toward him across the seat. That movement infects my mind with so much molten sexual heat that I can't help but moan. My legs drift slightly apart.

He reads my mind and slides his hand between my knees, grips my thigh, and then creeps a little higher. Everything he does erupts my desire out of my deepest soul. He's really touching me like that.

Making out with a man who's so much older than I am turns me on as never before. It feels so forbidden and otherworldly—and yet I feel totally safe with him.

His confidence and experience tells me loud and clear that he'll make sure to please me. He knows exactly how to turn me on. He doesn't fumble or doubt himself at all.

I don't have to worry about him hurting me or messing up or losing control. I let myself go with him. I can be vulnerable and turned on at the same time.

He slides his hand a little higher toward my panties. His mouth tears off mine and he presses his forehead into mine rasping through his teeth while he rubs me to dripping wetness.

I moan and rock back on the seat as he sends these blistering waves of passion and ecstasy through me. I want him to touch me. I want to feel him take me and make me show him how intoxicating he is.

He must already know how he affects women. Women melt for him everywhere he goes. He only has to look at a woman to make her weak in the knees.

He eases back a little more and his blue eyes spark with fire as he slides his fingers into my saturated channel. He sees every shade of drunken pleasure spasming in my features when he touches me like this.

"Spread your legs for me, baby," he husks. "That's right. Oh yeah, you are so damn hot. That's right. Show me how much you want this."

I can't stop myself. Maybe I'm one of the useless sluts who throw themselves at him, fool around with him once, and disappear into his past.

I don't care if I am that. I just want to feel this with him. I want to feel what it's like to be with a man who understands my body as well as he does.

I want him to use all his knowledge and experience to give me the most mind-blowing pleasure of my life. I don't want to pass up this chance even if it only lasts a few minutes or a few hours.

The limo will pull up to my apartment building any second now. I'll get out and go inside. Dante will ride off in his limo with my smell clinging to his fingers. That's all I am to him—a few minutes of masterful enjoyment before we go our separate ways.

He doesn't stop pumping his fingers into me. He brings my juices bubbling to the surface and keeps snatching scorching kisses from my lips.

He pulls back each time to look into my eyes and see how close I'm coming to the brink of madness.

"Come on, baby," he murmurs. "Let me hear you scream for me. You know you want it. Let me see how hot you are."

His words spark my desire off the charts. I can't hold back. I hike my dress up to my hips, prop my feet on the seat, and ride down on his hand as the surge of climax hits me. I scream out.

"Yes!" he yells over my screams. "Yes! Come on! That's it! That's right! Take it all the way!"

I can't stop. I throw myself down on his fingers, turn my head away, and whine and cry as a catastrophic orgasm splits me in half. I want so much more, but this is enough.

I love that he encourages me to show him how turned on I am. I give him my body for a few minutes of pleasure. I don't need or want anything else.

This is one of the most mind-blowing orgasms of my life—probably because he's so different from every other man I've ever been with. He's so much older. He's older than my father.

Thinking of him that way somehow makes him so much hotter and more appealing. It's taboo and comforting at the same time.

I want to turn over and give him an equally explosive release, but the limo pulls up to my building just then. The driver parks at the curb and leaves the engine running while I moan, writhe, and tremble with the last traces of pleasure flowing out of me.

Dante doesn't stop driving his fingers into me. He slows and then glides them in and out in dreamy, magical softness. My wetness coats his hand. I need to collapse. At least I won't have to do anything after this.

I'm still reeling in the stratosphere when he pushes me back, bends over, and buries his face between my legs. He devours my sensitive tissues and makes me scream all over again.

He sucks the juices off my flesh and licks me to tease me back to fuming desire, but he doesn't take me back to full orgasm. He just turns me on enough to make me ache for him. Then he sits up, pulls his fingers out of me, and starts pulling my dress down.

Now I really need to go upstairs, get into bed, and finish myself off. I'll be dreaming about him tonight for certain.

He pulls me upright, draws down my dress, and waits for me to pick up my purse. He gets out on the curb, opens the door for me to get out, and then moves over to the driver's window. "You can go home, Curtis."

"Yes, Sir, Mr. Helme," the driver replies and pulls away.

Dante turns around and locks his eyes on me. Did he really just say that?

His eyes tell me in no uncertain terms that he isn't finished by a long shot. He puts his hand behind my back and steers me toward the building.

Chapter 4: Dante

I step into the elevator with Emberlynn. She holds herself stiff and nervous on our way upstairs. She keeps making eye contact with me and looking away.

She's so attractive and hot. She probably has no idea how hot she is. Is that why I'm doing this—because she's hot—or because she relied on me to go to bat for her at the gala?

Is that really what I am? Am I one of those older guys who takes advantage of younger women just because I have the power and they're younger? I don't like to think of myself that way, but maybe it's true.

I do seem to attract younger women for some reason. Then again, I haven't met anyone my age that I'm compatible with. Most women my age are way over the hill and not even trying to do anything with their lives.

Their idea of growing old together is going on cruises and puttering around in the garden. They don't understand why I want to keep working—and they don't take care of themselves. What am I supposed to think?

It isn't like I go out of my way to seek out younger women. Some of them seek me out, but they don't appeal to me if they do.

Maybe that's what appeals to me about Emberlynn. She didn't seek me out. She wasn't even thinking of me in that way until things just changed in the limo. I wasn't thinking of her that way, either. It just happened.

Her eyes overflow with doubts and questions every time she does make eye contact with me. I want to reassure her—and I also want to touch her. I want to devour her.

She fires my blood like few women I've ever met—of any age. I want to consume her and conquer her—and I want to be gentle with her. I don't want to hurt her. I just want to give her the greatest night of sex that she'll never forget—and I want to have that with her, too.

All this talk about taking myself off the market—I still feel that way. I don't want anything permanent—but then again, I might if I found the right person.

I don't see how someone so much younger could be the right person, but we can have a good time while it lasts. That's all this is.

The elevator dings and she gets out at her floor. She fumbles with her keys and opens the door to a small apartment. The window looks out at the wall of another building next door, but the apartment is clean and comfortably furnished. It isn't dingy or rundown.

She decorates the open-plan living room with a crocheted blanket over the back of the couch. The blanket makes the place cheery and homelike.

She puts her purse and keys on the kitchen counter. She keeps fidgeting like she's really nervous. That makes her so much more appealing to me.

I want to soothe her fears, but wanting to soothe her fears turns me on like I can't believe. Everything about her turns me on.

She glances up at me and I ease over to her. I try to communicate through my eyes how much I want to take her right now.

I want to make her orgasm the way she did in the limo. I want to bend her over and make her a beast of raving desire. Does she even want that with me?

I lean in and kiss her. She kisses me back—and the passion starts to take over. She doesn't ease off when I touch her. She moans and then screams when I pull down the top of her dress and her bra and dive in to grab her breasts in my mouth.

She arches her back and thrusts her chest into my mouth and hands. She tastes mouth-watering—and not just her breasts.

I grab her in a frenzy. I have to have her. I'm in her apartment. She knows why we're here.

I scoop her up under her armpits and lift her to sit her on the kitchen counter. I grab her legs, push them up and apart, spread her thighs, and tug her panties down while I bury my face in her succulent flesh.

She moans and sobs in rising delight. Her fingers clench in my hair. She pumps her hips into my face faster and harder the way she pumped them into my hand. She's coming close.

I drive my fingers back inside her while I maul her ravenous greed. I growl at her and her juices gush onto my knuckles.

I glance up at her and see her breasts swaying outside her dress. Her thighs surround my face and her head lolls back in blurred rapture. Her lips pout open and she sobs and screams every time I lick her.

She rocks on the counter in such a sexually charged rhythm. She's going to climax right here in my mouth.

I grab her ass and crush her choice flesh in my hand. I have to have all of her. I have to feel her all over me and smothering me with her sweetness.

I take a chance and slide another finger into her on the next stroke. She screams once and then dissolves in a torrential flood of orgasms one on top of the other. She bucks and roars. Her fingers clamp in my hair and she pulls me in extra hard.

She throws back her head and her body convulses there in front of my eyes. She's gorgeous in the peak of climax. I want to keep her here and let her float in the clouds for the rest of the night.

I pull out when she starts to cycle down. She jolts when I lick her sensitive clitoris. She needs to power down.

I stand up straight, but she doesn't sit up or close her thighs. My instinct tells me to rip my pants open and drill her to the stars right here on the kitchen counter—either that or bend her over and pound the daylights out of her until she screams again.

Her eyes float open and she has to work hard to focus on me. She's so out of her mind that she barely sees me. I want to bring her back to earth so she knows what's happening before we take it any further.

She sits up, and before I realize what's happening or even think to stop it, she tumbles off the counter, sinks to her knees in front of me, and buries her face between my legs.

She starts off by nuzzling me through my pants. I'm already throbbing hard and straining to get at her, but she doesn't wait for me to do anything. She closes her mouth around my shaft through the fabric and starts jawing up and down the length.

I gasp and my hand flies to her head, but she turns me on so much that I can't bring myself to push her away. Does she even realize what she's doing to me?

She must. She can feel me spasming and twitching in her mouth. She yanks my belt open and unzips me while she drives me out of my mind.

I grab her shoulder to stop her, but she's already pulling my shorts down. My slab falls into her waiting mouth and she starts sucking the life out of me.

I stagger backward in shock at the heat and power of her mouth, but she only follows me on her knees. I slam into the fridge and flatten myself there from the unstoppable energy coursing through her.

She draws it out of me in such hot, powerful waves that I can't stop it. She flexes her fingers into my hips and angles her mouth back and forth around me to drain me of every ounce of my strength.

I can't stand this. I grip her shoulder too tight. I should stop her. I should pull her off. I want to be the one who does it to her, but this feels too good. No one has ever given it to me like this before. She's incredible.

She rises a little higher on her knees, grabs my hip, and pulls me to thrust into her mouth. I try to hold back, but I wind up grabbing her head and drilling all the way down her throat.

She moans in something like pleasure when I do that. She relaxes and opens her throat to take me as deep as I want to go.

I can't stop myself. My body takes over. I stand up straight, take hold of her head, and drive all the way in again and again as deep as I can possibly go.

She only moans louder and whimpers in what sounds like climax. She softens in my hands and lets me take what I need.

She doesn't stop for an instant, not even when I roar out in broken rapture and explode in her mouth. I don't want it to end like this. I want so much more, but she does it so expertly that I can't help it.

I collapse back against the fridge groaning in agonizing release. My knees almost give out from the intensity of all this pleasure and sensation rushing through me and out of me.

Does she want me to leave now? I don't think I can face that.

She doesn't give me a chance to collect myself. I'm still reeling in a daze when she stands up, takes my hand, and leads me stumbling into her bedroom.

Chapter 5: Emberlynn

I stop next to my bed and look up at Dante to make sure he knows where he is and what he's doing here. His eyes snap up to meet mine. He looked a little out of it in the kitchen just now, but he wakes up instantly when I bring him into my bedroom.

His eyes flash with a different kind of fire. He places his hands on my hips, turns me toward the bed, and moves in behind me.

Everything he does is so smoking hot. He can't even look at me without infecting me with so much sexual energy. Just his hands resting on my hips like this send shockwaves through my body and mind.

He slides his hands up and down my hips and sides for a minute—just to let me know exactly what he's thinking and what he's about to do.

He eases in behind me and his hot breath blasts into my ear. He rubs his body against me from behind so I can feel that he's as hard as ever even after just exploding in my mouth.

He grinds his hard shaft against my ass through the back of my dress. He knows exactly what he's doing and how to do it. He never leaves me in any doubt about what he wants—and what I want.

He's everything I want. He's more man than I can handle—but that's what makes him so intoxicating. I can't get enough.

He steps away, takes hold of my dress, and lifts it over my head from behind. He exposes my body in my bra and panties. Then he unclips my bra. He doesn't turn me around when he slides it off my shoulders and lays it aside on the floor.

I already know what's coming by the time he puts his arms around me, crushes my breasts in both hands, and then he takes hold of me in all his furious power. He doesn't hold back this time—if he ever held back.

One hand scrapes up to my throat, but he doesn't hold me that way. I almost wish he would.

He plants his hand against my chest to hold me in position and his other hand plunges into my panties to finger me to the ends of the earth.

I scream out as his touch charges my sensitive flesh, but he doesn't plan to let me off easy this time. He lifts me off the floor, tugs my panties aside even as he rubs me to screaming madness, and his iron rod finds its way inside.

I can't stop convulsing in his arms as he skyrockets me into outer space on one drilling climax after another. He never lets me come down between epic releases.

I disintegrate in his arms. I don't have to control anything or hold myself together. His powerful embrace does that for me. I'm in his hands—literally. I can completely crumble in these mindless throes of rapture that don't stop no matter what I do.

He carries me so far out in space that I might never come down. I hardly notice when he lowers me onto the bed, glides my panties the rest of the way off, and stands over me watching me thrash in life-changing pleasure while he takes his clothes off.

He's as powerfully built underneath as I knew he would be. Every muscle strains when he climbs onto the bed, raises one of my legs, turns me on my side, and plunges back into me pumping me full of all that endless pleasure.

I let it all go in that moment. I get lost in his eyes in those few moments when I can focus well enough to see him looking down at me.

He watches in master triumph that I'm completely at his mercy and yet experiencing the greatest bliss of my life. He knows exactly what he's doing to me. That's why he's doing it.

He stays in command even when he rolls onto his back and pulls me on top of him. He pushes me upright so he can watch me buck and ride him in wild frenzy. I can't stop as long as he stays hard and wants to keep doing it.

He finally lifts me up, scoots forward on his knees, and pins me against the wall at the head of the bed. He arches his hips and muscular abdomen into me to slam me into another mind-warping orgasm.

I can only cling to him and ride the waves as far as he wants to take me. I don't know when this will end, but I have to stay with him and experience all of this until it does end.

He wraps his chiseled arms around me as soon as it's over, collapses back onto the bed with me still strapped to him, and settles on his back with me on top again.

We both sink into deep kissing and soul-searching eye contact while the power fades between us, but the connection doesn't. He's beautiful inside and out. I could never regret spending the night with him, not even if this is the only night I get to spend with him.

He pulls my head down onto his shoulder and holds me while I finish gasping and quivering from all this delirious energy he's been giving me. He kisses the side of my head and then the side of my neck. He strokes my hair and rubs my back.

Everything he does is so comforting and casts such a heart-wrenching contrast to how much power and force he brings out during sex. He can be so tender and caring, but that doesn't make him weak or any less powerful.

I love that about him. I love how he's always in command of every situation. He never does anything without knowing that he can handle it and how to handle it.

I drift off lying on top of him like this. I wake up in the middle of the night lying on my side with him curled up around me. His arms hug me around my waist.

Searing heat blasts into me from his skin. He doesn't need blankets and I don't, either, as long as I'm lying this close to him.

I startle awake before I realize where I am and who I'm with. He tightens his grip and murmurs in my ear, "You're all right. You're safe at home in bed. It's just me. You're all right."

I collapse in relief when I realize who it is that's holding onto me. I have never felt safer with anyone. I fall asleep and wake up in the early hours of the morning. Dante is still there lying behind me.

He kisses the side of my head. "You slept a long time," he murmurs.

"Did you sleep at all?" I grumble.

He chuckles low in my ear. "I was enjoying myself too much. I didn't want to miss anything."

I shut my eyes and try to ignore the soft meaning in those words. "Something tells me you have meetings to attend today or something like that."

He buries his face in my neck from behind. "I do," he murmurs. "That's why I didn't want to miss anything. What about you? Do you have meetings today or something like that? Do you have to go to work?"

I sigh and roll onto my other side so I can face him. "I won't have any work until Ross calls me again—which means he'll probably never call me again."

"He can't do that. I told him not to mess with you."

"He doesn't have to fire me. He can just say he didn't need me. He'll bump me to the bottom of his list and leave me down there with the people he never calls again. If you ever ask, he'll just say he already had enough people and he'll call me for the next event. You won't be able to do anything to him."

He scowls at me. "That isn't right. He shouldn't be able to do that."

I kiss him once and sit up. "It was really sweet of you to stick up for me the way you did. I guess I'll spend the day putting in a few other applications and looking over the job listings. It's way past time I got another job anyway."

He rolls onto his back and looks up at the ceiling. "I sure wish I could find something for you. A lot of people at the club could use a good executive assistant—and you must be good if you made Marianne happy."

I laugh. "She was actually really great. I liked working for her."

"That's what's so impressive about it. She was so exacting about everything."

"She was, but she knew she was. She knew how hard she could be to please, so when someone did things the way she wanted them to, she was over-the-top complimentary—and she gave bonuses for good work, too. She was the best boss I've ever worked for—no question."

He looks over at me. "You're wasted working for Ross."

I shrug that away. "I'll have to get another server job to pay the bills." I kiss him one last time. I see the time of parting coming closer. "Do you want to take a shower with me before you leave?"

"You go ahead. I have to go home before my first meeting. I'm having dinner with my family tonight. I want to get a few things ready first. I'll take a shower there where I can change into my own clothes."

I smile at him and head off to the bathroom. It's such a relief that he and I can part ways with no expectations or hurt feelings or hidden agendas.

I don't expect anything from him. He's a billionaire businessman. Last night was never going to be anything more than last night.

I get out of the shower and we make breakfast together in my kitchen before he kisses me goodbye, thanks me for a wonderful time, and leaves.

Chapter 6:
Emberlynn

I wash the breakfast dishes, change the sheets on my bed, and put them in the laundry before I go out for the day. I go to the employment office first and check all the new job postings there.

I don't have to wait around for Ross to make his move. I already know what the outcome of last night's disaster will be.

I'm qualified for five posts at the employment office. I get on my laptop, do some research, and put in my resume and application for each job.

One of them is hiring for a project manager at Nightscape Holdings. It's the parent company of a chain of retail malls all over the country.

Nightscape Holdings owns a bunch of other businesses and shares in businesses, but they all relate back to retail outlets one way or the other.

I'm not as qualified a project manager as I am an executive assistant, but maybe I can convince the hiring team to give me a chance—or that my skills have enough crossover to pull it off. I apply anyway.

I leave the employment office and ride the subway across town to the public library. I don't need to come here to use the internet or anything like that, but I like to come here just to sit and think while I do research, study things that interest me, and soak up the vibes.

I head upstairs to the legal stacks. It's always quiet up here. Everyone who comes here also comes here to think, research, and soak up the vibes of quiet, studious, introverted peacefulness.

I pass the librarian's desk and nod to the tall young man standing behind the computer. Simon Whitmeyer is way too thin, way too tall, and his tie looks like it's choking him.

He smiles at me from behind his big, Coke-bottle glasses, but he's already talking to another man across the counter.

The other guy looks about thirty and he wears casual brown slacks, white sneakers, and a beige short-sleeved button-up shirt. This guy is much shorter and much bigger in the shoulders than Simon.

The guy has a compact, powerful energy like he's a fighter of some kind. His dark brown hair exaggerates his dark brown eyes.

I stop there at the desk and wait for the guy to finish talking to Simon. Simon gives me a desperate look, but I'm in no rush. Simon is my friend. I can wait all day for this guy to finish before Simon and I shoot the breeze and pass the time of day.

The guy glances over at me and takes a step back. "You go ahead," he tells me. "I'm being a problem child today."

"No, no! Not at all, Sir," Simon exclaims. "I can have it sent over by the end of the day tomorrow. I wish I could make it sooner, but the courier service only runs once a day and it already left the Bronx library today."

"I understand," the guy replies. "You don't have to worry about it." The guy turns to me and frowns. "Are you sure you don't want to go ahead?"

"It's fine," I tell him. "You finish whatever you need to do. I can wait."

"Are you sure? This might take a while."

"Take all the time you need."

"It doesn't have to take a while, Sir," Simon interrupts. "If you just tell me whether you want me to send the document over or not, I can put the order through the system.....or you can go pick it up."

"That's the problem," the guy replies. "I don't know if I want to have it couriered or go pick it up."

He smiles at Simon, but the situation unsettles Simon so much that he doesn't return that smile. He shuffles his feet. "What do you want me to do, Sir?"

I hold out my hand to him. "I'm obviously complicating things here. I'll see you in a little while, Simon."

"Uh....okay, Emberlynn," he stammers. "Bye."

I walk off into the stacks. He gets too flustered under pressure. I don't want to make it worse. He can work it out with the guy and catch up with me when no one else needs to talk to a librarian.

I spend another hour on my laptop, but I'm not accomplishing anything useful here. I go back out to the desk. The guy must be done by now.

He is, but another patron is talking to Simon now. I wave to him behind the woman's back and leave the library.

I stop off to talk to my friend Abdul at the hotdog stand on the corner. The same thirtyish guy is already standing there getting a hot dog from Abdul.

The guy looks up at me in between paying, getting his change, and then taking his hot dog. "Emberlynn, right?" he asks.

I smile at him. "That's my secret alias. I'm really a vigilante superhero called Nighthawk when the sun goes down."

He laughs and holds out his hand while he licks the extra mustard off the end of his hot dog. "I'm Lucas. Do you know that kid in the library?"

"Who—Simon? Yeah, I know him. He's a friend of mine. That's why I wasn't in a hurry to talk to him. I was just going to pass the time with him and chat. I wasn't there for a book."

"Oh, I get it. He's a nice kid—very polite. I respect that."

Kid?" I ask. "He's probably the same age you are."

Lucas frowns. "He is? He seems much younger."

"What are you—thirty? He's thirty-three."

"Oh, okay. I didn't know." He shrugs that away. "So what brings you to this part of town? Something tells me you aren't a lawyer."

"I'm not. I'm just a library vampire." I shoot him an evaluating look. "Something tells me *you* aren't a lawyer, either."

He laughs again. "I am a lawyer. Should I take that as an insult?"

"Not at all. I usually think of lawyers as either corporate sharks or penniless pro bono social justice desk jockeys who work for charities and grassroots organizations."

He won't stop grinning at me. He's really good-looking and he has a charming smile when he lets it show. "I'm one of the corporate sharks. I'm in disguise as my mild-mannered alter ego right now to throw my archvillains off my trail."

Now it's my turn to laugh. "Good one. So what's your superhero name?"

"Thundercloud," he tells me. "That's how I rain fire and brimstone on my enemies." He makes me laugh again and then waves to a park bench near Abdul's hot dog stand. "Do you want to sit down and talk—or do you have to fly off and rescue a plane that's about to crash?"

I can't stop smirking at him. Bantering back and forth and trading jokes is too much fun. We sit down. He sets his hot dog aside. He doesn't look like he's in any hurry to eat it in front of me.

"You didn't tell me what brought you to this side of town," he goes on, "besides sucking the blood of poor unfortunate paralegals you find in the stacks."

"I'm actually between jobs. I come here to get on my laptop, research new job posts, and apply for them."

He frowns at me. "That sucks. What's your area of expertise? What are you applying for?"

"I'm an executive assistant—or I was in my last job. I've been trying to find something else."

"What was your last job?"

"I worked for Marianne Talbot. You probably don't know who that is."

His jaw drops. "Marianne Talbot?! For real?"

I nod. "Did you know her?"

"Know her?! Are you insane?! I was never anywhere close to being in her league. I never set foot in the same room with her. Wow. I know a few people who are looking for assistants. I could put in a good word for you."

"Thank you."

He shoots me a look on the side. "I could pass on your phone number if you....you know.....if you would stoop so low as to give it to me."

I find myself laughing. "Are you saying you would pass it on to them or is that your way of asking me for my number?"

He spreads his hands and blushes. "I don't know. Would you go out with me if I asked you to?"

I can't stop smiling back at him. "I might if you asked me to."

"So....can I get your number?"

I tell him my number. He enters it into his phone and sends me a text. *Hi, Emberlynn. Will you go out with me on Friday night?*

I laugh and text him back. *Who is this and how did you get my number?*

He laughs, too. "I can see I have some ground to cover before we get to the first date."

"Isn't this the first date?"

His cheeks color and he tries unsuccessfully to hold back another grin. "Definitely not. This was a chance encounter in a park."

I stand up. "I better go get that plane before it breaks the sound barrier."

He holds out his hand to shake mine. "Don't get your cape tangled in the engines, okay?"

I laugh. "I'll do my best. I'm sure you'll hear about it on the news if I do."

He grins one last time. "It was really nice to meet you."

"You, too. Have a good day."

I walk off. He was nice. I wouldn't mind going out with him. His sense of humor makes me forget about all my other troubles. Maybe giving him my phone number will lead to me getting a decent job for a change.

Chapter 7: Dante

I walk into the conference room and shake hands with Jamal McLaughlin and Lacey Short. "Are you all ready, Dante?" Lacey asks me.

"I'm ready." We sit down on one side of the conference room table. "Who do we have first?"

"Evan Grant," Jamal tells me. "He comes from Dynamite Construction. His experience is in construction project management—which isn't exactly what we're looking for—but he does have a lot of experience with managing multiple large teams at once, project timelines, and budgeting. He's our most qualified candidate."

I check my watch. "We have another seven minutes before his interview. Let's go over his resume and see about...."

My assistant Suzie sticks her head in just then. "Evan Grant is here for his interview."

"He's early," Jamal murmurs.

"Both of his references call him a go-getter," Lacey adds. "He could be our guy."

"Send him in, Suzie," I tell her. "We'll see him now."

The three of us stand up when the door opens a second time. Evan Grant is a young black guy. He looks barely a day over twenty-four, but he's actually twenty-three. I normally wouldn't dream of hiring someone so young, but his record speaks for itself.

He's almost as tall as I am and he looks like he works as hard as his construction guys. He wears a nice grey suit tailored to his muscular shoulders, but he still comes off as a construction guy wearing a suit.

He shakes hands with all of us. "Thank you for considering me for this position," he tells us. "I know my experience is in another industry, but I'm confident I can adapt my skills to any project."

"We're confident in your abilities, too, Evan," I tell him. "Sit down and let's talk about this."

He sits down. The muscles of his legs bulge through his pants. He's a powerful guy—not the kind I usually meet in my line of work.

"What made you apply for this job?" I ask. "I'm sure you could get as much work as you wanted in the construction field."

"I could. That's the problem. I started as an apprentice when I was fifteen. I worked my way up to being project manager of my company. I don't want to get stuck there. I want to switch to something corporate so I can keep rising." He locks eyes on me. "The truth is I applied for this job because of you, Mr. Helme."

"Me?!" I exclaim. "Why me?"

"Your reputation for cultivating your people and training them up the corporate ladder is legendary in the business world. I want that. I need it. I don't have as much education as some, but I can learn anything and I'm willing to do whatever it takes. I'll go as far as you let me go. I just need people who will believe in me and let me run with it. If I take this job, I want it understood that this will be a bridge to something bigger—something higher and more challenging. I don't want to get stuck in the same role for the rest of my life—which is what I would be doing if I stayed where I am."

I exchange glances with Jamal and Lacey. I've heard enough, but we still have a stack of interviewees to get through today.

Jamal and Lacey ask Evan a few more questions about what he expects from an employer, what his salary expectations are, and a few more probing questions about his management style and what he would bring to our organization.

It's obvious from listening to him that he knows a lot about managing people. The amazing thing is that he learned it all in the field. He has no education beyond a high school diploma and he barely got that.

He's so unbelievably smart and driven that I can't help but be impressed. I tell him so when we shake hands. I tell him he is definitely on our short list even though he's our first interviewee of the day.

I sit down. "Wow. I don't know about you guys, but I think we just met our new project manager."

"He certainly is impressive," Jamal adds. "His comments about needing cultivating, supportive employers were awe-inspiring."

"Let's see who else we have. Then we can make a decision one way or the other." I sit down and flip to the next employment folder in my stack of applicants.

I freeze when I see the name at the top. *Emberlynn Rhinehart.* My mind goes into a tailspin thinking about that night. I didn't know she applied for this job.

The HR department screened the applicants, contacted all their references, and created a list of interviewees for us. I hesitate to open her folder. I shouldn't be interviewing her—but no one knows I spent the night with her.

Excusing myself now would give too much away. I would have to explain to Jamal and Lacey why I don't think I should interview Emberlynn.

I can get through the interview and let Jamal and Lacey make the decision. I can just stay quiet on the subject of Emberlynn and go along with whatever they decide.

She didn't say anything that night about having project management experience. We have a few minutes before she's due to show up for the interview. I take the time to flip open the folder in front of me.

She doesn't have project management experience—not the kind we're looking for. She doesn't even have project management experience in another industry the way Evan Grant does.

She shows up ten minutes early. Jamal tells Suzie to send Emberlynn in early, too. I stand up to meet her.

Her eyes bore into my soul when we come face to face across the conference room table, but she shows no sign that she recognizes me.

I don't, either, except that we can both see it in each other's eyes. We both remember that night. It would be kind of hard to forget it.

I shake hands with her. "Thanks for coming, Emberlynn."

"Thank you for considering me." She shakes hands with Jamal and Lacey and we all sit down.

Jamal starts things off and says what we're all thinking. "I don't think I have to tell you that we're looking for someone with more direct project management experience," he tells her. "You worked as an executive assistant to Marianne Talbot which is impressive on its own, but it isn't the kind of experience we're looking for."

"I might not have gotten the job title of project manager, but I did manage teams, projects, timeframes, and budgets," Emberlynn returns. "I was responsible for overseeing all of Marianne's operations managers, keeping them on timeframe and within budget, and also hiring and firing new employees—as well as managing Marianne's schedule and her timeframes and budgets. I know I'm probably not the conventional applicant you thought you were going to get, but I have the skills and experience to manage any project of any size—and any team or organization of any size. I managed Marianne's organization for seven years. I don't know what experience could better prepare me for this role."

Lacey asks a few more questions about Emberlynn's experience with Marianne. It becomes obvious after just a few minutes of talking that Emberlynn is telling the truth about managing Marianne Talbot's organization—which is a herculean feat in itself.

I stay out of the conversation. Emberlynn's eyes shoot to me a few different times during the interview, but I don't say anything and she doesn't challenge me to get involved.

Jamal jumps in and the three of them wind up having a lively discussion about Marianne and Emberlynn's experience working for her.

Emberlynn answers every question effortlessly. She can explain everything in a way that makes it clear she knows what she's doing.

"Well, I'm stumped," Jamal tells me after Emberlynn leaves. "I really can't decide which of them is better."

"I can tell you right now which one I think we should hire," Lacey replies. "I think we should hire Evan."

"How can you say that?" Jamal asks. "Emberlynn obviously knows her stuff. Neither of them has direct industry experience, but I bet you they could both do the job equally well."

"That's exactly why I think we should hire Evan," Lacey replies. "Don't you remember what he said about needing an employer who will cultivate him and train him up the ladder? Emberlynn never said anything like that."

"None of us asked," Jamal points out.

"It might still have come up in conversation," Lacey counters. "Emberlynn didn't quit working for Marianne because Emberlynn wanted to move up and out in the world. Emberlynn would have been very happy to work as someone else's executive assistant probably for another seven years. She only stopped because Marianne died. I didn't hear any of that kind of life-affirming drive from her. My money is on Evan. He could become an executive with that kind of fire in his belly. Emberlynn would always be an employee no matter what her job title."

Jamal frowns. "You make a good case."

Lacey turns to me. "What do you think, Dante?"

"I'm torn between them, too. There's no doubt in my mind that they could both do the job, but if you think Evan's drive and ambition make him the better candidate, then I can go along with that."

"So can I," Jamal replies. "I guess if they're both equally matched in every other area, then that one factor should tip the scales in Evan's favor."

We spend the rest of the day interviewing ten other candidates for the position. One of them does have direct industry experience in exactly the field we need him to.

The guy has a lot of experience, but all three of us develop an instant dislike for the guy the minute he walks through the door.

Jamal, Lacey, and I meet up at the end of the day. The final decision comes down to Evan or Emberlynn.

We all agree that the two applicants are equally matched in experience, expertise, and in their ability to adapt their current skillset to the job at hand even though neither of them has ever done the job before.

Lacey is absolutely adamant that Evan is our man based solely on his passion to keep developing and growing even beyond this role. He doesn't want to stay in the role long-term—and that makes him so much more valuable.

Lacey is so bent on this and Jamal and are on the fence about the two candidates. I really don't see the difference in every other area of their offerings, so we decided to go with Lacey and hire Evan for the position.

Chapter 8: Emberlynn

I sit at a corner table where I can look out the coffee shop's front windows. I can watch people passing by and pigeons pecking on the sidewalk.

I put my laptop on the table next to the flag with my order number on it, open my laptop, and check my emails for any replies on my recent job applications. I have a few replies and offers for preliminary interviews—nothing exceptional.

I have gotten a few inquiries from businesspeople and executives who want assistants. I'm meeting them in the next two weeks.

The waitress comes over and I have to move my laptop aside so she can put my hot chocolate down on the table. I smile at her. "Thank you!"

She smiles back and returns to the counter. That's when I see Dante Helme standing there with his back to the room. He's ordering a cappuccino to go.

I'm still sitting there glued to my chair when he turns around. He freezes when he sees me. Will it always be like this? Will we both always go deer-in-the-headlights when we see each other even at a distance?

He stares at me like he's going through the same inner turmoil. The barista distracts him by giving him his order just then. He has to turn his back on me to pay for it.

I look down at my computer. He'll leave and I don't have to see him again. No big deal. We couldn't expect to live in the same town without seeing each other occasionally.

I'm just starting to put him out of my mind when he comes over to my table. "Do you mind if I join you, Emberlynn?"

I look up at him. "Um...okay...if you want to."

He pulls out the chair opposite, sits down, and takes the lid off his cup. "How have you been?"

"Pretty good," I tell him. "You look like you're doing good."

"I am." He smiles at me. "Did you find a job yet?"

My smile evaporates. Is he trying to imply something? "No, I'm still looking."

"I'm sure you'll find something soon. You're so qualified."

I stare at him while he takes another swig of his drink. He takes one of the paper napkins from the table and wipes the milk foam off his upper lip.

He sees me watching him. "If you aren't doing anything, would you like to go out this weekend?"

I stiffen. "Why do you ask that?"

"Because I had a good time with you the other night and I want to see you again."

"Do you mean you want to have a good time with me again? Because if that's the reason, I'd rather skip it. I'm not a pit stop for you to make when you have nothing better to do."

His jaw drops. "I wasn't trying to imply that at all! I meant that we would go out—like really go out."

I look away. "I don't think that's a good idea."

"Is that because we hooked up once? Is that why you think it isn't a good idea?"

I spin around fast. I shouldn't even be talking to him—especially about this. "Why didn't you hire me as a project manager?"

"What?!" he gasps. "Do you think I'm asking you out because of that?"

"Maybe you are. Did you turn me down for the job because you're interested in me—or because you wanted to keep sleeping with me—and you didn't want anyone from your work to find out about me?"

"NO!" he practically yells and struggles to keep his voice down. "Listen to me. The position came down to you and one other candidate. None of us had any problem with your experience or your skills. You convinced all of us that you were perfectly capable of doing the job."

"Then why didn't you hire me? Because I would much rather have the job than go out with you."

I realize too late how resentful and injured I sound—and I guess I am. I probably could have gotten that job if anyone else in the world had interviewed me.

He fights his voice down even lower and barely chokes out in a strained, husky murmur, "Listen to me. You could have gotten that job and you could have done it incredibly well. There was never any doubt in any of our minds that you were perfectly capable of doing the job—not ever. The other candidate didn't have direct industry experience, either, but he did have one thing going for him that you didn't. It all came down to that." He swallows hard. "If it makes you feel any better, I cut myself out of the decision entirely because I didn't think I could be objective when it came to you. I was totally on the fence between you and the other candidate. I was not the deciding voice in rejecting you—not at all. Lacey was the only person who had a very strong opinion about which of you we should hire and she convinced the rest of us to go along with her opinion. That's all."

I don't want to believe him. "So what was it? What did the other candidate have that I don't?"

He takes a deep breath. "I'll only tell you if you promise not to get offended. I'm speaking on behalf of Lacey here. I'm going to tell you what she said. I'm not saying this is what I think."

"But you just said she convinced you—so you must think she's right."

He raises both hands. "It's like this, okay? The guy is a twenty-three-year-old black kid from the South Bronx. He barely finished high school and he started as a construction apprentice when he was fifteen. He worked his way up to project manager using nothing but his wits and iron determination not to stay at the bottom for the rest of his life. Now he's pivoting out of construction into the corporate world because he doesn't want to be a construction boss his entire life, either. He only took the job on condition that we cultivate him and train him up the ladder so he can become something bigger. He says he applied for the job especially so he could work with me because he knows I cultivate my people to grow and move up in life. He says he needs that."

"What makes you think I wouldn't want that? Do you think I want to be an executive assistant all my life? You could have cultivated me."

He spreads both hands. "You didn't say in the interview that you wanted anyone to cultivate you. That's all I'm saying. He was very specific about it. He was firm and direct that he wouldn't accept anything less. That was his whole reason for applying for the job. You say you don't want to be an executive assistant your whole life, but you probably would have stayed one if Marianne survived. You would still be an executive assistant seven years later with no ambitions to move on or up or sideways or anywhere else. You could have transferred to any industry in those seven years and gotten paid ten times more and had a thousand times the opportunities with your experience—but you didn't. You got comfortable. That's the argument Lacey made—that you would always be an employee no matter where you went or what role you filled. This guy is a tiger. He would never be an employee—not even if he became an executive running the whole damn company. He would never be comfortable—in anything. There is no limit to what he could become. That's why we hired him—for what he could become and what he said he wanted to become. You never said you wanted to become anything. You never made any comment one way or the other to show that it ever crossed your mind to be more than an executive assistant. Right now, you're applying for a bunch of executive assistant positions when you could be so much more. You could have gotten hired a long time ago if you kept applying for project manager positions."

I look away. I don't want to hear this—because he's right. I never wanted to be anything else. I never let myself break out of my comfort zone.

I never thought about being anything other than an executive assistant—not until right this very minute. I only applied for the project manager position because I was desperate for a job. I never really wanted to do that or anything else.

I never really wanted to be an executive assistant, either. That's the real truth. I only did it because it was a job.

I stare at my computer. What exactly do I want to do? I've never really thought about it. I wouldn't even know where to begin to answer that question.

Dante notices my reaction right away. "I'm sorry if I offended you. That wasn't my intention at all. I shouldn't even have been the one to interview you—but I thought it would cause you more embarrassment if I tried to explain why I shouldn't be interviewing you. I thought it would be better if I just stayed quiet and let someone else make the decision—which is what happened. You wouldn't have gotten the job even if I hadn't been there at all."

I should have known he wouldn't use the interview to mess with me. He doesn't play those games. Business is too important to him and so is his integrity as a businessman.

I force myself to look up. "I'm not offended by what you said."

"I'm sorry if I offended you by asking you out. I would never treat you as a pit stop. If you don't want to go out with me for real, then I can only respect that and gracefully back away."

"Why *do* you want to go out with me?" I ask. "Aren't I a little young for you?"

He bursts out in laughter and his cheeks color. "You clearly haven't seen the kind of girls who follow me around trying to get me to go out with them."

"Can't you find someone your own age to go out with?"

"No," he replies. "I can't find someone my own age to go out with. I've tried. Believe me. No one my age understands why I still go into the office every day when I could be sitting on a beach in the Bahamas instead—and even fewer of them want to get together with someone who still goes into the office every day instead of sitting on a beach in the Bahamas instead."

"Why *do* you go into the office every day?" I ask. "You have enough money to retire to a beach in the Bahamas."

"I go into the office every day because I enjoy it. I go into the office every day because the challenge of running my business keeps me energized and motivated to stay alive. Did you know that the average life expectancy after retirement is six years? Six years! I will never retire. Why should I—so I can play golf and sit on a beach in the Bahamas? I can't imagine anything more boring. I'm already living the life I want to live. My children and family and my children's families are all here. Running my business and staying active in the club keeps me going. I would disintegrate if I retired. I might as well lock myself in the funeral vault right now if I'm going to do that."

I stare at him across the table. We've never talked this much—about anything. I don't know anything about his life—or I didn't until now—not anything more than what I've heard in the news or seen in magazines and articles on the internet.

He had enough money to retire more than thirty years ago. He just keeps working harder and getting more involved with every passing year. He doesn't show any sign of slowing down.

There are men in The Billionaires' Club who are younger than he is who look and act thirty years older than he does. They already shuffle around like old men. None of them has his energy and none of them are as engaged with other people as he is.

That's the thing about him. He engages with everyone. He engages with the lowest dishwasher in the back room of every gala. He talks to them, smiles at them, learns their names, asks questions about their lives, and compliments their work.

He notices everyone. He doesn't check out—ever. He never turns the lights off and he never lets off the gas—not ever.

Is that what I've been doing? Have I ever put the gas down on anything—ever? I can't imagine living his life—because I'm not as switched on as he is.

I look down at my computer. I'm not sure what to do on it now.

Chapter 9:
Emberlynn

"But enough about me," Dante goes on. "What have you been doing since I saw you last? What are you doing to pay the bills if you haven't found a job yet?"

I cringe. I'm ashamed to say it now. "I'm working as a server in another catering company. Ross still has me on his books, but I'm picking up other shifts elsewhere."

He studies me across the table. He doesn't say again that I could be doing just about anything else if I only applied myself.

He looks away first and says, "I'm sure you'll find something soon."

I open my mouth to say something and stop myself. He notices that, too.

"What?" he asks. "I won't ask you again to go out with me."

"Maybe....maybe you could do something else....for me......if you want to....."

He perks up. "Like what? What do you want me to do for you?"

"Maybe you could....you know....help me....."

"Help you with what?"

"Help me....you know....not be an employee."

His eyes shoot open. "Really? Is that what you want?"

I shrug. "I don't know what I want. I never really thought about it—but you're right. An employee is all I've ever been. I don't know how to be anything else."

"There's nothing wrong with being an employee. The whole world needs employees."

"But clearly you value those who are not employees more than those who are. Those who are not employees get paid more...."

"That doesn't make them better."

"It just makes them more valuable to the marketplace. Isn't that what you're saying—that the only difference between me and this other guy was that I'm an employee and he isn't—so you hired him because he isn't one? So if I am one, I'm less valuable than someone who isn't."

He shrugs. "I guess if you want to put it that way, then yeah, I supposed you're right."

"So could you show me how not to be an employee?"

He smiles and actually blushes this time. "I wouldn't know that because I've never been an employee. I've always been like this."

"Like what?"

"Okay, well, for a start, you know the expression that you always work for yourself, right?"

I stare at him. "What do you mean? I've never worked for myself."

"Okay, well, that's the problem right there. You never work for someone else—ever—even when you have a job where someone else is paying your paycheck every month. You always work for yourself no matter what you're doing. If you're waiting for someone else to pay your paycheck, then you're an employee. You cease to be an employee when you start working for yourself even if someone else is giving you the money to pay your bills. You're either working to build your own thing on the side or you're working within the company to make it your own."

I frown. "How would I make it my own?"

"Well, like this young man we hired to be our project manager. I'm quite certain he doesn't plan to stay a project manager any longer than we absolutely make him. He'll start infecting the rest of the company with his tentacles, finding out how it works, and start taking over the place."

My jaw drops. "And you let him?! You actually let people do that?!"

"Of course. Those are the most valuable people to have around. They take ownership of their jobs and even the company itself. They come up with ideas to make the company better, how to solve its problems, and how to serve the customer better. Those are the people who start as apprentices and wind up becoming company CEO one day. They don't get that way by waiting for someone to give them a paycheck. They start doing it the minute they get hired. They start doing everyone else's job for them and they do it ten times better. That's how they get promoted. They come to me or one of the other executives and say, 'Hey, I know a way we can do such-and-such an aspect of the company better.' Then the new person takes over so-and-so's job and starts doing it until, one day, they do the same thing to the company CEO—and presto! They got the job."

"So....you would actually want that? You would actually be happy if....say.....this kid took over your job?"

"Of course. I would think it was the greatest thing ever—because it would be the best thing for the company."

"But you would be out of a job then! How could you be happy about that?"

"I only have a job because I'm the one who keeps coming up with those ideas. Most people underneath me are more than happy to let me take the top spot and assume all the responsibility and come up with the ideas. I would love it if one of them came up with an idea or if this kid—as you call him—came to me and said he knew a way to do my job better than I do. I would be the first to step aside and tell him to let it rip."

I blink at him in stunned disbelief. No one has ever talked to me like this before. I look back down at my computer. Now what am I supposed to do? The idea of working for myself....I never thought about it before.

"What do you think you might like to do?" he asks.

"I....I don't know...."

"Well, you should probably think about it. Maybe that's why you haven't gotten a job—because you don't really want to do it and it's coming across in interviews."

"Is that what happened when I interviewed with you?"

"No, not exactly. It's just that this kid had a level of enthusiasm and.....and ownership. Yeah, that's the right word—ownership. He took ownership of the job, himself, his career path—he owned it all and he was proud of it. Nothing was going to stop him from doing what he set out to do—not us, not his background—nothing. He knew exactly what he had to do and how to do it. He was very specific about why he wanted that job and why he wanted to work for that company in particular. He had a reason to do it and he was on a mission to do it. He would have done it even if he didn't get the job. Those were the very first words out of his mouth. You never said anything like that in your whole interview—because you aren't on a mission and you don't have a reason. That's why Lacey was so set on hiring him—because he had that and you didn't."

I don't know what to say. I can't think about this—and yet I have to. I have to figure this out. No one has ever challenged me to think about this before.

He sees my reaction and downs the last of his drink. "I can see I've said too much. I better go. It was good to see you again. I hope I see you around sometime." He stands up to leave.

"Dante!" I call after him.

He turns around. "Yeah?"

"I....I would like to see you again....sometime.....if you want to.... you know....not as a pit stop....but for real.....if you want to...."

He bursts into a smile. "I would love that. I can get your phone number off your job application. Would that be okay with you?"

"Yeah. Sure."

"Great. I'll get in touch with you. Bye."

"Bye."

He walks out of the coffee shop and waves to me on his way past the window before he passes out of sight. I look down at the computer.

What does working for myself even mean? I can't even form a concept of what that means.

It means taking ownership. That's what he said. It means taking ownership of the company, the business, the job—as if they were my own.

I never did that with Marianne—or with anyone else I ever worked for. I always knew I was running the business on behalf of someone else.

I always knew the buck stopped with someone else. I didn't have to care about the end result because that was always someone else's job. It didn't matter if it didn't work out because that was someone else's problem. I was always just an employee.

I don't know what that means, but I can't go back to being someone else's executive assistant. I don't know what I'll do instead, but I have to think of something. I can't go back to the way things were before this moment.

Dante's words break something between me and the past. I can't keep doing the same thing I have been doing. I can't be an employee anymore.

He said he's never been an employee. This young man he hired has never been an employee, either. They realized the truth and followed a different road to get where they are.

They're at the top of the food chain now. Dante is already there and this young man is obviously on the fast track to getting there.

I'm checking the employment listings and waiting for someone to give me a paycheck. That's the difference.

I open my documents folder and click on the file labeled, *Resume*. I stare at it for a long time and then push, *Delete*. The file disappears. I'll never submit my resume again. Something needs to change.

I'm still working for the catering service to pay the bills. I stare at the empty place where my resume used to be. I'll keep working at the catering service, but I make myself a solemn vow right then and there. This will be the last job I ever have. Period.

I'll never apply for a job again. I'll never submit my resume. I'll never ask for anyone's permission....ever....again.

I shut my laptop, leave the coffee shop, and set off walking back across town toward my apartment. What will I do instead? I could do literally anything. I have no reason to do one thing over another.

What do I even enjoy? What am I even passionate about? I don't have any passions or hobbies or outside enjoyments. I better come up with something—and fast.

Chapter 10:
Dante

I open the door to my penthouse apartment and a whole crowd of people mob me through the entrance. My daughter-in-law Tracey rushes me and kisses me on the cheek.

"Hi!" she calls over the noise and shoves a baking dish into my hands. "Green bean casserole, right?"

"My favorite. You're my hero." I hug her with one arm, but her kids are already grabbing me and shoving her out of the way.

My grandson, Todd, and granddaughter, Evelyn, drag their mother away so they can hug me. "I brought the glider, Granddad!" Todd tells me.

"What are you going to do—fly it to the next building?" I ask. "You'll never get it back."

"Granddad—I won the schoolwide spelling bee," Evelyn tells me.

"Great. You can start proofreading my business documents for me."

She laughs and she and her brother go out onto the terrace where my brother Aiden, his wife Roxanne, their son, Mark, his wife Delia, and their three kids are already hanging out and making themselves at home.

The kids swim in the pool. Mark and Aiden stand at the barbecue while Mark turns burgers and sausages on the grill. Roxanne sits at the picnic table cutting up vegetables to make a salad while Delia polices her children in the pool.

My son Jay follows Tracey and the kids into the apartment. Jay hugs me. "Hey, Dad," he mumbles.

"How you doing, son?" I ask. "Are the patients behaving themselves?"

He laughs. "*They* are. It's all the viruses and bacteria that keep misbehaving. I need you to come in and give them a lecture for me."

I pat him on the back and carry the green bean casserole to the kitchen. "That's your job, son. That's why you get paid the big bucks."

"No one gets paid bigger bucks than you."

"I don't get paid to talk to viruses and bacteria. I don't speak the language."

He squints through the sliding doors leading out to the terrace. "It looks like everyone is already here. We're late."

"Not everyone," I tell him, and right then, the apartment door opens without anyone knocking. My younger son, Lucas, walks in and splits in a grin when he sees me and Jay standing together in the kitchen.

"Hey! My two favorite people!" he chides and comes over to us.

Jay puts his arm around his brother's shoulder. "Sorry, brother. You've been dropping down the list these last few years."

"I sure hope I have." Lucas grins at me. "Hey, Dad."

"Hey, son. Did you check out those documents I sent you?"

"I did. I have to wait for the library to transfer over a few precedent case files from the Bronx. Then I'll be able to answer your questions."

"You aren't going to spend the whole afternoon and evening talking business, are you?" Jay counters. "We're here to enjoy ourselves."

I wave back and forth between my two sons. "Why don't you ask Lucas to say a few bad words to your bacteria and viruses? He's good at straightening out evildoers, repeat offenders, and bad guys."

They both laugh. "Don't put me up to dealing with viruses and bacteria," Lucas counters. "People are bad enough. I don't deal with the archvillains of the world—although I did meet a caped crusader the other day. She was gorgeous."

Jay and I both laugh. "You two should team up," I tell him.

He grins back at me and his cheeks color. "I plan to."

I grab a few bowls of side dishes from the fridge and take them out to the picnic table on the terrace. My sons hang back and talk on the way out there. Lucas is the only other single man here besides me.

Todd and Evelyn strip off their clothes. They're already wearing their swimsuits underneath. They drop their clothes on the pavement and dive into the pool.

Tracey goes around picking up their stuff and moving out of range so the kids don't splash water on their clothes. Delia moves her kids to the shallow end of the pool. They're younger than Todd and Evelyn.

Todd and Evelyn keep getting out, climbing onto the diving board, and cannonballing into the deep end. They create giant waves that splash up onto the pavement.

Delia is doing enough policing of the kids. The rest of us can relax at the picnic table and shoot the breeze until it's time to eat.

My family all asks me about what I'm doing, how I'm doing, what I'm up to, and everything about what social events I'm planning for The Billionaires' Club.

Each of my family members has his or her own career and interests outside of work. Lucas is the only person here whose professional life intersects with mine.

He and three of his college buddies all went to law school together. They all studied corporate law and they formed a law firm together right out of college. They take a lot of clients from The Billionaires' Club.

Lucas knows almost everyone in the club. They're all either former or current clients of him and his partners.

My companies use him and his partners, too. It doesn't always work for me to hire my son as our company lawyer, so some of his partners represent us when we need someone else.

He and his partners are the best in the business. My companies wouldn't use them otherwise. No one even comes close. Everyone in the club knows it. That's why the members all use him, too. He's the only option if you want to get the job done right.

Lucas and I wind up talking about our mutual acquaintances, his cases, my work, and cases and jobs my company has in progress with his firm.

The others talk about other things. Mark and Delia talk to Jay about their kids' ongoing allergy situation. All three of Mark's and Delia's kids have the same allergy panel. No one can figure out the cause because neither Mark nor Delia have any allergies.

Jay is their family doctor, so he's been intimately involved in the whole saga. In a way, Mark and Delia do the same thing with Jay that I do with Lucas. Jay has a set of skills and expertise that Mark and Delia need—just like Lucas has a set of skills that I need.

It would be stupid not to use those skills when he's the best there is. Some people call it favoritism. I call it hiring the best man for the job. I don't give a damn that he's my son.

Actually I do give a damn that he's my son. I couldn't be prouder of both my sons. Jay has a beautiful family. I couldn't be prouder of him.

Lucas will have that soon, too. He just needs to find the right woman. He'll make a great husband and father. I'm certain of it.

Maybe this caped crusader he mentioned is the one. He sure looked delighted when he mentioned her. I haven't seen that sparkle in his eye for a long time. She must have been someone pretty special.

The kids get too tired of swimming. Their mothers move in to dry them off and get the kids changed back into their regular clothes. Then we sit down to eat.

We lounge in the living room shooting comments back and forth after dinner. Delia, Roxanne, and Tracey clean up the dishes and pack the leftovers in plastic containers to take home to their own houses. There's more food here than I can eat by myself.

I get a message on my phone while we're sitting there. I look down at a text from Jamal. He's sending over Evan Grant's employment contract for my approval.

That's when I notice another message from Suzie. She's sending me Emberlynn's phone number like I asked her to.

"Do you have a hot date, Dad?" Lucas teases. "Who is she?"

I turn bright red and don't look up from the phone. "It isn't a date. She's just a young lady who wants me to coach her in business."

"What's her business?" he asks.

"She doesn't know. That's the problem. She doesn't know what she wants to do."

"Text her back and ask her out," Jay tells me and both my sons laugh at me.

I grin at them and bend over my phone. "Mind your own business."

They elbow each other. "When are you going to go out with someone your own age?" Mark asks me.

"Find me someone my age and I'll go out with her," I tell him. "Just make sure she doesn't expect me to sit on the couch watching daytime soap operas with her—and make sure she works out. Those are my only two requirements. Call me when you find someone."

He shares a smirk with both of my sons. The three of them are always trying to set me up with someone. The problem is that they can never find anyone who is compatible with me.

Most of the time I don't even hear if they found someone they want to set me up with. The ladies in question hear about my work schedule and say I'm not for them. The very few times I do hear about it, I'm the one who says I'm not for them for exactly the same reason.

I respond to Jamal by telling him I'll sign the papers tonight and send them back to him by tomorrow morning. Then I thank Suzie and log Emberlynn's phone number into my phone.

I send her a text. *How is it going? I hope I didn't overload your brain at the coffee shop today.*

It was fine, she replies. *It's just giving me a lot to think about.*

What do you think you might do?

I have a few ideas. I'll run them by you when I see you next.

Why not run them by me now since you're here and I'm here and we're all here.

Very funny. I haven't really pulled them together into a clear idea, but I will. I should have something definite for you soon.

Do you need funding? How will you float your idea off the ground?

I have some ideas about that, too. You definitely gave me a lot to think about.

I want to help. I want to get involved if you think that would help you.

I want to see how much I can do on my own first. I will ask for help if I need it, but the truth is that I've never even tried to do anything on my own before. I want to see how much I can do. I want to stretch myself and find out how much I'm capable of. Then I'll ask.

Okay. I'm here if you want to talk.

I really appreciate everything you said today. I really appreciate that you were candid and told me what I needed to hear. You changed things for me today.

For the better, I hope.

I think so. I don't know how it will all play out, but you definitely helped change my thinking from employee to....well, whatever this is.

That's great. I'm glad you're thinking that way. You could be doing so much more than applying to be someone else's assistant. You have resources and strengths you've never tapped.

I guess that's the point. I haven't tapped them and I need to tap them before I call on someone else to help me. I need to find out how deep these resources go and how much I can actually do. I have a feeling I can do a lot—a lot more than I realize.

I get it. I'm here if you need anything at all. Don't hesitate to tell me if I can do anything.

I won't. Thank you again.

I'll let you get back to it. I'll talk to you later.

She texts, *Bye,* and a smiling face emoji.

I put my phone down and see my sons, my nephew, and my brother all watching me.

"She must be something pretty special," Lucas remarks.

I look away. "Maybe."

"Are you gonna ask her out?" Jay asks.

I grin at him and wind up blushing. "I already did."

They hoot and elbow each other again. I laugh. They can enjoy themselves at my expense. I don't mind.

My nonexistent love life has been a subject of family jokes for a long time. They like to poke fun at me whether I'm going out with someone or not.

I'm sure my sons wouldn't find the subject nearly so entertaining if I was going out with someone in a steady relationship. Then it would become boring to them and whoever she was would become just another member of the family like Tracey and Delia.

I have to stop myself from texting Emberlynn back to ask her to go out with me. I don't want to pressure her. I need to slow the train down before I run it completely off the rails. I feel myself heading there with no way to stop it.

Chapter 11:
Emberlynn

I sit down in the coffee shop across from Dante. It's been a week since I last saw him. We've been texting back and forth, but he still hasn't asked me out—not officially.

This is just a casual conversation in a coffee shop. This isn't a date or anything.

We've been talking about business—what he calls entrepreneurship. He has a lot to say about it. It's a world I know nothing about. I have a lot to learn and a lot of catching up to do on people like Evan Grant, the young man he hired to be his project manager.

Dante has focused all our conversations on just developing me in my own thinking about myself as the CEO of my own private enterprise. That's what he calls it even though he's talking about my life.

He encourages me to think about my life as a business with income, expenses, assets, and liabilities. I'm the CEO in charge of all the strategic decisions. It's up to me to decide where the company goes, what it produces, and how it grows.

I never thought about my life like that before. It's a whole new dimension in reality I never imagined.

He smiles at me across the table. He's already drinking a cappuccino. "Do you want to get anything?"

"I'm okay. I just had breakfast and coffee at my apartment, so I'm ready to go."

"So what do you want to talk to me about?" he asks. "Do I get to find out what your secret project is now?"

I take a few deep breaths, pull a tablet out of my purse, and turn it on in front of him.

"So after we talked last time, I was thinking about what you said about the skills and strengths I developed when I was with Marianne—running all her projects and events and stuff."

"Yeah?" he asks. "Those are all the skills we would have used to hire you as a project manager."

"Yeah, I know. That's what got me thinking to do something similar to that—because I already have all that experience. The only difference is that it wasn't mine—because I always knew Marianne was the one holding the bag at the end of the day. See?"

"Right. So what's the project?"

I switch on the tablet. "Okay, well, you know Marianne did conventions. She organized corporate events, comic book conventions—all that kind of thing."

"Yeah? Are you thinking to take over from that?"

"Not really—but I am planning to do something similar." I navigate on the tablet and show him a series of slides including promotional posters, schedules, and a bunch of documentation. "I booked Madison Square Garden. I'm organizing a concert festival with forty different bands performing over a week. I have vendors, food concession stalls, merch for the event and all the acts, accommodation for the bands, promoters signed up, and a bunch of investors on the line."

His mouth falls open and his eyes glaze over. "You booked.....Ma dison....Square Garden....."

I laugh from nerves. "What do you think?"

His eyes dip to my tablet. I show him the event poster with the top-billed bands listed on it. I'm calling the festival The MegaDome Experience.

I flip to the full line-up, the schedule of events, contests, raffles, and other entertainment including comedy and performance acts sprinkled throughout the week.

He shuts his mouth, gulps, and takes the tablet out of my hands. He flips through all the documentation, including emails from a few investors and promoters getting on board and expressing their excitement.

I also have letters from the senior organization managers at the Gardens telling me how much I need to pay to book the Gardens for a whole week. I booked a time slot for two years from now.

I try not to let the number overwhelm me. I have to at least break even—and that means paying all the bands and performers, charging the vendors and concession stallholders, paying to get the merch produced and selling it, hiring security and emergency medical personnel, arranging with the Police Department—everything.

Dante hands back the tablet and looks away. He won't make eye contact with me. "Wow," he breathes. "This is huge."

"I've never done anything this big before." I hear my voice shaking. "What do you think? I have to pinch myself to really believe it's real. I don't know if I can do this."

"You're already doing it. You already booked the Gardens and lined up the bands. You're already soliciting investment. You're doing it. You can't back out now."

My hand flies to my forehead and I laugh again when I get butter-flies in my stomach. "Don't remind me."

He stares deep into my eyes. "I never imagined you could do some-thing like this. This isn't what I had in mind when I told you to work for yourself."

I try to shrug and wind up squirming. "I didn't think it would get this big. It just kind of....happened."

He puffs out his cheeks. "Well! What do you need me to do? You seem to have this in hand."

"Do you think I can do it? Do you think it's too much?"

"You're doing it. Just grab the reins and ride that horse to the finish line. That's all you gotta do."

"I don't know if I can."

"You have to. You're doing it. You're making it happen. It looks like you're covering all your bases."

"Do you think so? You don't see anything I'm missing?"

"Do *you* see anything you're missing?" he asks. "Something tells me you've been thinking about this nonstop for the last week."

I laugh again. "Yeah. I have."

"If you haven't thought of anything you're missing, what makes you think I can? This is your business. You know it so much better than I do."

Now I'm the one who has to put my eyes back in their sockets. "My business! This isn't a business! I don't have a business."

"Sure, you do. You're a promoter—or maybe more like an executive producer. Your business is this event—and anything else you decide to promote after this. You're producing this event. You're responsible for seeing that it turns a profit—so you better crunch the numbers."

"That's what I've been trying to do." I flip to a spreadsheet. "This is my itemized list of all my expenses, both known and unknown, and projected income. I'm keeping a tally of how much I need to make to pay all the expenses—as well as the percentage I'll have to charge for all the merch—all of that—so I turn a profit and maybe have enough to pay myself when this is all over."

He spreads his hands and leans back in his seat. "Okay, sweetheart. You convinced me. I don't need to see that."

"But that's why I need you. I need you to check it over and make sure I didn't miss anything."

"You check it over and make sure you didn't miss anything. I'm not your boss. You're the boss. The buck stops with you—not me. You're the one who is carrying the bag here. If the numbers are wrong, you're the one hanging out to dry with the bill. That's what working for yourself means. I didn't sign up to take the place of your boss."

I stare at him as the hammer comes down. He's right. I'm the bottom line here. If I don't check the numbers and make sure this works, then I have no one to blame but myself for the consequences.

I can't solicit investors unless I'm willing to put my name and my ass on the line for this project. Thinking that scares the ever-lovin' shit out of me.

It also excites me like nothing else I've ever experienced. I'm doing this. The minute I think that, all my doubts evaporate. The numbers are right. All my preparations are right. I've been checking them around the clock for the past week.

I switch off the tablet, stuff it into my purse, and fold my hands on my lap. "Okay."

He blinks at me. "Okay what?"

"Okay, the numbers are right. I don't need you to check them because I already did."

"That's it?" he demands. "Just like that?"

"Yep. They're right. I'm certain they are. MegaDome will turn a profit—a big profit. In fact, this might even make me a millionaire."

His mouth falls open. "Are you sure?"

"Yep. I'm sure. We can talk about something else if you want to. I don't need you to check it. How are things going with you?"

"Um...." he stammers. "Things are going good for me. I've just been....you know....taking care of business, hanging out with my fa mily....."

"Tell me about your family. Who do you have? You said they were all here in New York."

"I have my brother, his wife, their son, his wife, and three kids. So that's my nephew and his three kids. Then I have two sons, one of whom is married with two kids."

I beam at him. "Aw! You're a grandpa! That is so sweet."

He snorts at me. "Don't say that. You make me sound really old."

"So what do your sons do?"

"One is a doctor and the other is a lawyer."

"So are they employees?" I tease.

He makes a face. "My older son, the doctor—he definitely is. He doesn't have an entrepreneurial bone in his body. His talents lie elsewhere—but he's an excellent doctor. He's very caring. His patients love him. They invite him and his wife over for dinner and holiday parties all the time. He's practically a member of all their families."

"Wow. That's incredible."

"My other son, the lawyer, is entrepreneurial. He and his buddies have their own firm. They're doing really well for themselves. I'm proud of both of them."

"What's the story with their mom? Is she out there in the world somewhere?"

He looks down at his drink. "No, she died a long time ago when my boys were six and eight. I've been on my own with them ever since."

My blood runs cold and my smile evaporates. "I am so sorry. That must have been so hard. I shouldn't have made a joke about that."

"It's okay. It's ancient history."

"Have you been in any relationships since?"

"Nothing that has lasted more than a few months—so I guess the answer to your question is no, I haven't been with anyone."

I cringe. "That sucks. I'm sorry."

"Don't be. It's just the way it worked out and my boys came through it. They made it and they grew up to be men I can be proud of. It was hard at the time, but it was worth it to give them the life they deserved."

"You must be proud of yourself, too, if you did all of that on your own."

"I am proud of it. I'm very happy with my family the way it is. My younger son will settle down soon and then our family will get even bigger. It isn't like I have to get with anyone because everything I wanted to accomplish in a relationship is already happening."

I study him on the side. "I can see how you might feel that way."

"What do you mean?" he asks. "What other way is there to feel about it? I'm a grandfather. It isn't like I could ever have any more kids."

"It's just strange to think about it because I'm on the other end of the spectrum. I haven't gone through all of that yet. It's all in front of me and it's all behind you. I could never see it like that unless I went through it myself."

"You'll get with someone and you'll see how it is."

I watch his face while we talk. He still hasn't asked me out again. Will he ever? Maybe he's given up on the idea of going out with someone so much younger. I can see how that wouldn't really work. We're in completely different stages of life.

I make up my mind not to think about that. His guidance and support with this new venture is more than I could ask for. I need that a whole lot more than I need to go out with someone.

Now isn't the time for me to be going out with someone anyway—not when I'm biting off so much more than I can reasonably chew.

"So tell me more about this whole business thing," I prompt. "What's today's pearl of pithy wisdom?"

"I'm going to pretend you didn't just used the word, 'pithy' in a sentence," he teases.

I laugh. "Come on. Drop your wisdom in my ear, oh wise grandfather."

He turns bright red, but he won't stop grinning. "I already did. You already saddled up your bucking bronco. You're already sitting in the saddle and holding onto the ropes. Now you just have to ride the damn thing and pray to Almighty God that it doesn't buck you off before the bell."

"Except that I have to ride it for two whole years—not eight seconds."

"Welcome to the world of business. You did all this. You can't complain about it now."

"I'm not complaining. At least I have time to take care of everything. I have time to print all the T-shirts and order all the merch and hire all the sound technicians and everything."

"Are you all set for advertising, promotion, and all of that?"

I nod. "I have a series of radio spots going out for the whole year leading up to the event—and also poster distribution, internet advertising, and social media campaigns."

"Don't forget to promote to the rest of the Eastern Seaboard—not just the NYC area," he tells me. "You want to market heavily in New Jersey, Upstate, the whole maritime region, and anywhere within reasonable driving distance of Manhattan. People will come from all over to attend this—but only if they find out that it's happening. Don't leave anything to chance."

"Wow. I didn't think of that." I pull out my tablet and make a few notes.

"You might also think about booking a bunch of the surrounding hotels," he adds.

"I'm doing that. I have to put up the bands and other acts within walking distance of the venue."

"I'm not talking about them. I'm talking about all the spare rooms in town. You can book them, pay for them, and then sublet them to people coming in from out of town. You can make a lot of money doing that whenever a concert or some other big event happens at the Gardens."

I stare at him in shock. "You can actually do that?! Is that legal?"

"It depends on the policy of the particular hotel. You have two years. You can check the hotel policies, see which ones allow it, and book the rooms now. No one else will be booking them because no one knows about the festival. You'll get a low rate and maybe make two or three times as much by scalping the rooms the month or even the week before. A lot of people do it that way as soon as they find out about the event."

"Wow. That sounds incredible." I make a note of that, too, and then look up at him. "Anything else?"

"Go out with me on Saturday night—if you aren't too busy."

I laugh. "Okay. Twist my arm."

"Are you sure you can fit me into your busy schedule? I don't want to interfere with any of your meetings or investor negotiations."

I turn bright red. "The good news is that it's far enough in advance that I make my own schedule. I'm sure I'll be working around the clock when the time gets closer."

"You're doing great work here," he tells me. "I'm incredibly impressed. If I had known you were capable of something like this, I definitely would have hired you to be my project manager."

I wince. "I hate to break it to you, but I can make a lot more money doing it this way—and I'll be honest with you—working for myself is becoming addictive. I never knew it could be like this."

"I know what you mean." He squeezes my hand across the table. "Eight o'clock Saturday night? Will that work for you?"

"That would be great. I'll see you there."

He stands up, bends across the table, and kisses me before he leaves the coffee shop.

Part of me wants to take out the tablet and start poring over my notes, preparations, spreadsheets, and every other thing I have to do to get ready for this event.

I don't need to do that because I've already thought of everything. I have plenty of downtime now, but I won't when the time comes. He's right. Doing this is like riding a bucking bronco.

I've never been more grateful to have someone like him in my corner. I couldn't do this without his support. I don't need a boss telling me what to do and checking up on me, but I do need that.

Chapter 12: Dante

I come out of the elevator in my office building parking garage, get into my car, and pull out onto the street. It's getting dark and the streetlights are just coming on.

I'm driving home thinking about something completely different when I spot Emberlynn heading for the subway station down the block.

She's coming out of the print shop. Is she printing out posters for her concert festival. I can't believe she's actually doing this.

She's so creative and driven and talented. She really stepped up to the plate in a massive way. I hardly recognize her as the same person who was serving drinks at The Billionaires' Club gala.

I'm about to look away and drive on when two guys jump out of an alley next to the print shop. They grab her and drag her into the alley. No one else is around. I'm the only person who notices.

I react on impulse, yank my car across three lanes of traffic, and actually gun the engine to barrel into the alley. The guys are just pushing her against the wall, holding a knife to her throat, and covering her mouth to stop her from screaming.

She stares at them with huge eyes. Her whole body goes rigid in terror. She tries to plaster herself harder against the wall, but they're already holding her down too hard.

She doesn't see the car, but they sure do. They both turn. Neither of them knows what to do before I storm out of the car and barge toward them. It's a good thing they break and run for it. I would probably tear them limb from limb if I got my hands on either of them.

I stop in front of her and glare at them disappearing over the wall at the end of the alley. They're already gone.

She stares up at me panting in terror. She doesn't seem to see me until I turn around and look at her. I realize a second too late that I'm glaring at her now, too. I'm so enraged I can't stop myself from glaring at something.

"Are you okay?" I ask.

She gasps a few more times and then turns all the way around, puts her head against the brick wall, and bursts into tears.

I grab her, pull her into my arms, and hold her while she falls apart on my chest. She howls with sobs and her whole body trembles and quakes.

I find myself shooting death scowls in all directions. No one better hurt her—not while I can do something to stop it.

No one comes. We're all alone here.

She cries for a long time. I don't want her to keep standing out here in this shitty alley. It will only remind her of what just happened.

I pull her toward my car. "Come on," I murmur. "Sit down here. I'll drive you home. Everything's okay. They're gone. You're safe."

I put her in the passenger seat, buckle her seatbelt for her, and shut the door. I get behind the wheel and take a minute to pull a packet of tissues out of the glove box before I drive off.

I don't try to comfort her or talk to her on the way to her apartment. I don't know where to park when I get there. Her building doesn't have a garage, so I park in a parking lot down the street.

She stops crying on the way. I sit in the parking spot and wait for a while until she stops blowing her nose and checking her makeup in her compact mirror.

I finally squeeze her hand in her lap. "Are you going to be okay?" I ask.

She nods down at her torn tissue. "Thank you. I don't know how to tell you how grateful I am that you showed up when you did."

"Hey, what's a knight in shining armor for?" I smile at her. "I just want to make sure you're safe and protected. I could never let something like that happen to you."

Her mouth starts to twist up again. I don't want her to dwell on this. I get out of the car, open her door for her, and take her hand on the way into her building.

She doesn't let go of my hand in the elevator. I take her up to her apartment. "Could you.....?" Tears streak down her cheeks when she faces me outside her door. "Could you....please.....stay?" She breaks down crying. "I don't want to stay alone."

"Of course," I murmur. "Of course. Anything you need."

She tries to thank me, but no sound comes out. She forms the words with her crooked lips and then has to turn away to unlock the door. She lets me in, switches on the light, and then locks every deadbolt in existence to barricade herself inside. She's still scared and that's okay.

I pull her down on the couch. She's so jumpy that I can't stand it. I lean back on the cushions and ease her down on my chest. I run my fingers through her hair and rest my lips against the top of her head.

"You're going to be okay," I tell her. "You'll get through this and put it behind you. You're nervous and agitated because it just happened, but it will pass. You're going to be okay."

She slips her arms around me and squeezes. She buries her face in my chest and doesn't try to break away. She huddles in my arms where she feels safe. That's okay. I want to be this protection for her. I want her to feel this safe with me. That's what I'm here for.

I sink into the couch and prepare myself to stay here all night. I have nothing waiting for me but an empty apartment on the other end.

That's the moment when I realize I don't want to go home to an empty apartment. My life is full of family, but my apartment isn't. I live there alone. I've been alone for years—decades, even.

I lived with my boys for almost fifteen years after my wife died, but I spent most of the later part of that time by myself. My boys grew up, got independent, and spent more time on their own or going out with their friends.

Then they both went to college and left home. I've been alone ever since.

I never noticed it before this moment right here. I don't want to live alone anymore.

Maybe that's why it never worked out between me and any other women I dated. Maybe the problem was never the age difference or the fact that they weren't businesspeople or because they wanted me to work less.

Maybe the problem was me. Maybe the problem was that I really just didn't care about having someone in my life. I didn't need someone in my life. Having someone in my life or not having someone in my life—it was all the same to me.

Not anymore. I want *her* in my life—and not just in my life. I want her in my house. I want to be with her—for real. I wouldn't even mind living here in this tiny apartment with her. I don't give a damn where we live as long as I'm with her.

I scoot farther down the cushions and rest my head against the arm of the couch. This is where I belong—with my arms around her. I don't need to be anywhere else. I'm already home—as home as I'm ever going to get.

The sun goes the rest of the way down and the world falls into darkness outside. She doesn't try to pull out of my arms. She eventually falls asleep there.

I take out my phone and answer some emails from Lucas about our most recent corporate contract that he and I are working on together. He sends me over a version for me to look at.

We trade a volley of texts about certain clauses he thinks we should change and why. He also tells me his opinion on changes the other party wants us to make that Lucas thinks we should resist changing.

His mind works in mysterious ways. He thinks of things and sees things I never thought of.

He makes a few more changes to the contract and tells me he'll send it back to the other party's lawyers for review and further negotiation before we do the final sign-off. I've never been more grateful to have him as my lawyer—or one of them.

What are you still doing up, Dad? he finally asks me. *It's almost eleven o'clock at night.*

Oh, yeah. You're right. I didn't notice.

You should get to bed, he tells me. *You aren't as young as you used to be, you know.*

You better stop that. I can still put you in your place if I have to.

What are you going to do? he asks. *Send me to my room?*

I could try.

I would love to see you try that. Now go to bed or I'll send you *to your room.*

I have to stop myself from laughing so I don't wake up Emberlynn, but I'm going to be waking her up anyway.

I heave off the couch. "It's time to go to bed, sweetheart. Come on. You'll be more comfortable there."

She's still half-asleep, so I pick her up, cradle her in my arms, and carry her to the bedroom. She opens her eyes when I put her down and start taking her clothes off.

Her eyes drill into me with such power. I remember that look from the night we spent together. I guess this is turning into that—and I don't try to stop it. I want it.

I unpeel all her clothes. She sits up and moves her body around so I can slide her pants off and unclip her bra. She finally crawls into bed all naked. I take off my clothes and get in next to her on the other side of the bed.

She slides against me and her warmth envelops me. This feels so blissful and right. It isn't about sex. I want her heart—and it looks an awful lot like I already have it.

She wraps her arms around me, compresses her luscious breasts and stomach against my side, rests her head on my chest, and drapes her milky, satin thighs over my legs. She's already wet.

I run my fingers through her hair and kiss the top of her head. This feeling breaking me apart right now—is this love? Is it the beginning of what could become love?

She responds to me kissing her hair by tipping her head up to face me. Her eyes take hold of me. I have to kiss her, and before I know what's happening, I'm rolling her onto her back, crawling between her legs, and finding my way deep inside her hot, delicious darkness.

She kisses me for the ages. Falling into her depths feels inevitable. We rock together in a slow, steady, cosmic rhythm that doesn't end at the slippery boundary where our lips and tongues meet.

She wraps her arms and thighs around me taking me all the way into that heart of blessed togetherness. I don't have to be anywhere else. I do have to be here. I have to stay here.

She claws up my back, squeezes my neck, and threads her fingers through my hair. Her joints turn to butter in my hands. Her body sways when I beat into her. Her mouth sags open in blissful moans when I thump all the way into her deepest roots.

Her eyes float open in the fathomless wastelands of wordless connection beyond anything I could ever describe. She's right here in front of me.

This pleasure I'm feeling right now—it comes from her heart. Her body isn't really here at all. Her heart communicates so much more of what passes between us.

Her eyes tell me she feels it, too. Is this love? We're definitely together. I don't know what that means, but we're together in any and every way that counts.

We don't attack each other the way we did before. We explode into each other in screaming passion and then fall back into the same dreamy togetherness of just holding each other afterward.

I can't fall asleep once we both settle down and she rests her head on my chest. I find myself staring out the window and floating in my thoughts.

Her voice drifts into my mind from somewhere. "What's going to happen now?" she asks.

"What do you mean?" I press my lips against her scalp and rub her back. "You'll probably fall asleep....and I'll eventually fall asleep."

"I mean what's going to happen between us?"

"What would you like to happen between us?"

"I mean how would it work with you advising me on this festival if we're going to keep messing around like this?"

"How would that affect the festival? First of all, do you want to keep messing around like this—and how would it affect the festival if we did?"

"You weren't advising me because we were messing around—at least I hope you weren't."

"I wasn't. I didn't think you wanted to mess around anymore."

She stiffens. "This isn't why I asked you to stay."

"I know, but it happened anyway. I don't see that it affects the festival at all. It isn't like us spending the night together will stop you from planning it."

"You know what I mean. You can't advise me if we're going to be fooling around on the side."

"Why not? And why would we be fooling around on the side? I would advise you and support you if we were in a relationship, wouldn't I? Why shouldn't I do the same thing now?"

Her head shoots up. I have to loosen my arm so she can roll backward to look at me. "Relationship?! You want a relationship?!"

"Is that so surprising? Don't sound so horrified by the idea."

"I'm not horrified! I'm just surprised."

"Why are you surprised?"

"This is just casual. That's what I thought you wanted."

"Is that because it's what *you* want or because you think that's what I want?"

"You never asked me out after that one time—I mean you didn't ask me out when you said you were going to. I thought you were moving on from that idea."

"But I did ask you out."

"Not until much later. I thought you changed your mind and weren't interested."

"Well, I am interested. Are you? Is that what you want?"

She looks away and winds up staring at the ceiling. "I don't know. I never thought about it. You're....well....you're Dante Helme. I'm no o ne."

"You aren't no one. You're beautiful. You're smart. You're resourceful and talented and sensitive and caring. I don't see anything about you that I don't like." Now I'm the one who hesitates. "Is there anything about me that you don't like—or that you don't want to get involved with? Let's talk about this."

"I mean....you're so much older than I am."

"It doesn't bother me. Why should it bother you?"

"Because I might want to have children someday. You already said you're on the other side of that and it isn't like you could ever have any more. You're a grandfather. Your children would be younger than your grandchildren. It sounds so....so....."

I laugh. "Go on and say it. Don't spare my feelings."

"Well.....it sounds so *Deliverance,* doesn't it?"

I burst out laughing. "You're right. It does, but you said you *might* want children. Do you or don't you?"

"I don't know, but how do you answer that if I did? I care about you and I like you and I can see that you care about and like me, too, but that's all the more reason why we should care enough to let each other go and get together with people who can actually make us happy. We obviously can't make each other happy. You could never give me the life I want and I wouldn't be happy with you. I would only make you unhappy because we would both know we weren't what we want. See?"

"But you don't even know if you want children. You might decide you didn't, in which case you would have no objection to me—unless you really have some objection to the age difference between us. You don't seem to have a problem with me physically."

"I don't. How can you even say that? I mean....look at you."

I laugh. "I'm not as good-looking as you are."

"Please," she sneers. "I don't have a whole bunch of hot guys chasing after me trying to get me in the sack."

"Neither do I."

Now she's the one who bursts out laughing. "Stop that. This is serious business."

"You're the one laughing about it."

"Go out to dinner with me," I tell her.

"Aren't we kind of skipping a step here?"

"All the more reason we should go out to dinner on a real date and make it official."

She raises her eyebrows at me. "Official? You make it sound like you're going to propose to me."

"We'll just keep talking about it. We don't have to decide anything or making any sudden changes. Besides, the next two years are going to be crucial for you. I don't want to get in the way of that. We can take it slow and see how things play out."

Chapter 13: Emberlynn

D ante rolls over in bed and kisses me. He lies on top of me naked in my bed, but he doesn't try to do it with me—not again. We've been doing it off and on all night in between kissing and talking about different aspects of our lives.

"I have to go to work, baby," he murmurs. "It's Saturday today, so I'll pick you up at eight for our dinner date." He kisses me some more. "Stop kissing me. I have to go."

"You're the one kissing me." He kisses me some more and then laughs.

He sits up on the edge of the bed, does something on his phone, and goes to get in the shower. I stay in bed. I don't have to get up today—not until it's time to go out to dinner with him. That isn't for another ten hours. No way will I get up now.

He comes out of the shower, dries off, and starts getting dressed. "Listen to me, baby," he tells me while he pulls his pants on. "I want to introduce you and your festival idea to The Billionaires' Club. I know a few people who might want to invest in it."

I spin around. "Really? Who?"

"Giovanni Nowaczyk, for a start. He's big into entertainment. Some of the others might want to get on board with promoting it or just investing. What do you say? I can get you invited to one of the club meetings as a guest. You can rub elbows with everyone and talk business."

"Um....okay. Is that allowed?"

"It's more than allowed. It's encouraged." He stares off in another direction. "Actually, we're all attending a business conference at the end of the month. We can do it there. A few other investors and interested parties will be there. You can meet them at the same time that you meet the other club members. I can introduce you and you can run your idea up the flagpole."

"Thank you," I exclaim. "That sounds great. Outside investment is going to become more important as things escalate."

He bends over and kisses me. "Stay there. Don't get up. I'll see you tonight. Catch up on sleep. I don't want you falling asleep in your spaghetti."

I laugh and he lets himself out of the apartment. I get up and relock all the doors after he leaves. Then I go back to bed.

Spending the night with him leaves me totally relaxed and at ease with the world. I don't feel jumpy or skittish after almost getting mugged yesterday. He erases all of that and makes everything all right again. He's really good for me.

Now we're going out to dinner tonight and he's getting ready to introduce me to investors who might be interested in my concert festival project.

I never expected him to support me this much. I don't want to let him go. I just don't know if we have what it takes to go the distance—or even if that's what I want from him.

I don't know what I want—from anyone. I'm too young to decide on any of that.

Getting into a serious relationship with someone when I'm about to embark on the most hectic and stressful two years of my life—that sounds like the worst idea in the history of bad ideas.

Tonight is just a dinner date. We're just talking about it. It isn't a lifetime commitment—as he would say.

I fall back to sleep and wake up at four in the afternoon. I lounge in bed for another hour and stare out the window.

I can't stop myself from mentally running through all the details and preparations for the concert festival. I have almost all of them committed to memory. I don't even have to look at my tablet to go over them.

I really have thought of everything—and I have two years to stress about it if I haven't. I can always make adjustments later.

Dante has been drilling that into my head all this time. Doing business isn't about having everything figured out ahead of time. It's about making a plan, going with it, and pivoting on the move.

It's like driving. That's what Dante says and now I understand what he means. It's about making constant adjustments, adaptations, and course corrections to steer the ship or car or horse or whatever to the right destination.

I get up at five, take a shower, and get ready to go out to dinner. I have some time to go over my documents and review everything. I do some research on the local hotels and their subletting policies.

Then I research and bookmark other advertising channels in New Jersey, Upstate New York, and other Atlantic states where I would want to promote MegaDome farther afield. The project is all coming together.

Doing this work distracts me from what might be my nervousness about meeting Dante for dinner. I'm calm and ready to go by the time he knocks on my door and eight o'clock.

Going out to dinner like this with him feels like we're already in a relationship—and I suppose we already are.

We're going out. We're spending the night together. We're sharing each other's lives—or he's sharing mine. I don't know as much about him, but I'm finding out about him slowly but surely.

He takes my hand and leads me downstairs. We get into the limo with Curtis the chauffeur.

"Is this your car?" I ask Dante.

"No, my car is the Miata I was driving last night. I hire this limo when I don't want to drive—which is a lot of the time when I'm going to and from work and I want to do things on the way. That's most of the time. I don't drive very often."

"Why were you driving last night?"

"I don't know. I just feel like driving sometimes. Sometimes I like to drive out into the countryside—just to take a drive and clear my head. I can't do that in the limo. I use the limo when I don't want to waste the time by paying attention to the road. I can answer emails or take phone calls or review documents in the limo while Curtis drives."

"That makes sense. So does Curtis come with the car?"

Dante laughs. "Yeah. I request him especially because I like him, I know him, and I trust him to drive well. There are a few people who work for the same company that I don't like or trust and I would never drive with them again for any amount of money."

The window into the driver's compartment happens to be open right then. Curtis laughs. "We won't name any names, will we, Mr. Helme?" he calls back.

"No, we sure won't. We don't have to because we both know who I'm talking about."

Curtis laughs again and doesn't interrupt our conversation again before he pulls up to the curb in front of the restaurant.

Chapter 14: Emberlynn

C urtis the chauffeur opens the door for Dante to get out first. He offers me his hand to help me out.

He tells Curtis to wait for us in the parking lot around the corner. Curtis says, "Yes, Sir," and drives off into the night. Dante leads me into the restaurant.

He's reserved a booth in the back where we can have some privacy. We both slide into the benches. "This place is really nice. I've never been here before."

"I'm glad I could give you a new experience." He takes my hand across the table. "I'm really happy to be here with you. I'm thrilled with the way you're developing in this new project of yours. You're exceeding my wildest expectations."

I beam at him. "I had a lot of help along the way. I'm really grateful for your support."

"Always. You have it in any way I can give it. You only have to ask and it's yours."

"I'm not so sure if I'm ready to start meeting and greeting and rubbing elbows and talking business with a bunch of billionaires, though."

"Why not?" he asks. "I'm a billionaire and you've rubbed a lot more than elbows with me."

I laugh and wind up blushing. "That's different."

"How is it different? I mean, you won't be spending the night and having sex with them—at least you better not be—but that's exactly my point. You'll just be talking to them, showing them your documentation, letting them see your numbers, and they can decide for themselves if they want to invest in you. I bet you get at least a few takers."

"I don't know about that. I did some research into the membership after you left this morning. Giovanni Nowaczyk is the only member of the club who specifically does entertainment...."

"They're all always looking for businesses to invest in. They don't need to be doing entertainment as their own primary enterprise. They invest in other things that aren't their primary enterprise."

I frown at him. "Are you sure?"

"I think I would know. A bunch of us invested in Derek Salazar to help him make his comeback after he lost everything and built it all back up again. He would have come back without our investment, but he wouldn't have come back as fast as he did. We got him off the ground and now it's paying off for all of us who backed him. The guys are always looking for up-and-coming business that need help or that just promise to pay off in the end. You'll be talking to some of the female billionaires, too, I'm sure."

My head snaps up. "Female...billionaires...."

"Don't tell me you didn't know. What about Melody Gottlieb? She's a billionaire and she's a member of the club. She isn't the only one. Why are you staring at me like that? You know there are women in the club. It isn't a fraternity or anything."

I force myself to look away. "I guess I don't know as much about the club as I think I do."

"Well, you're going to have to learn."

"Do you mean because of you—because I'm....well, it looks like I'm involved with you, doesn't it?"

"I didn't mean that. You don't have to be involved with me if you don't want to be. I meant because you'll probably get investors from the club. I would be very surprised if you didn't. I wouldn't introduce you to them as someone I was involved with. That wouldn't be appropriate."

"How would you introduce me? How would you tell them how you know me?"

He shrugs. "I would tell them that you applied to work at my company, but we gave the job to someone else. I would tell them that you asked me to mentor you in business and I did and that's how you started this whole project—which is all true. They don't need to know about all this other stuff."

"But one of the billionaire club members could walk through that door right now and see us together. Then they would know we're involved with each other—or whatever this is that we're doing."

He squeezes my hand and beams at me. "Let's call it a business meeting."

I'm just starting to smile at him when, almost like it was meant to happen, someone walks past our table at that moment. I barely glance up in time to see a woman glancing down at me at the same time.

We recognize each other a split second before she walks down the hall heading for the bathrooms.

"Oh, no!" I groan.

"What's wrong?"

"That woman.....she's my best friend Rita."

"Oh, that's good. You can introduce me."

"It isn't good! I just said someone from the club might recognize us and now she definitely recognized us sitting here holding hands."

I start to pull my hand out of his grasp, but he only grabs it and holds onto it. "Let her see. I want to go out with you—like seriously. I don't want to hide in the shadows. I want the world to know we're going out together."

"Are you sure about that? Would you want your family to know you're going out with someone so much younger than you? What about your sons?"

"They've seen me going out with women your age or even younger. That isn't new."

"But you never got serious about any of them. I'm sure they wouldn't approve of you getting seriously involved with someone who might even be younger than they are."

"I don't care if they approve. I approve. That's what matters. I like you and I want to get involved with you—seriously—romantically. I want you in my life and I want to be in your life—even more than we are now. I don't want to hide it. I want us to be for real."

I look down at his hand, and right then, Rita comes back out of the bathroom.

She knows exactly what to look for this time. She sees me and Dante sitting there holding hands. She doesn't look away until she walks past us.

"She isn't much of a best friend, is she?" he remarks. "She didn't even say hi. You could have introduced me."

I have to use my other hand to cover my eyes. "She knows who you are," I mumble. "She knows exactly who you are. I can just imagine what she'll say the next time I talk to her."

"You'll tell her that we're involved. You'll tell her that we're in a serious relationship. She can't possibly object to that. The age thing isn't really a valid argument. If that's the only reason she or anyone else objects, then that isn't really a reason, is it? It's a vote in favor if it's anything because it means the person has nothing to say against the relationship itself."

"She can't say anything against the relationship itself because she doesn't know anything about you except what she reads in the press."

"Then what are you worried about? She might be able to talk if she got to know me or something and decided I was an asshole or a user or just a lecherous old man who wanted a much younger woman to use for my sick pleasure...."

I burst out laughing. "Will you stop all that?"

"Well, think about it. If she says the age thing is the only problem, then that's an admission that there is no problem."

"Is that what you plan to say to your sons?"

"Yes, exactly. I'm a grown man. I think I can get together with a woman as long as she's over the age of legal consent." He pretends to frown at me. "You're over the age of legal consent, aren't you?"

I can't stop laughing. "I'm pretty sure. I was the last time I checked."

"Then where's the problem?"

"I guess there isn't one."

"You're damn right there isn't one."

The waiter comes and we go through the rest of the meal talking about his business and mine. That's what I am now. I'm in business for myself. I can hardly believe it, but it's true.

I know a lot about Nightscape Holdings. I had to research it when I applied for the project manager's job. I just didn't realize at the time that he was the CEO of the parent company that owns Nightscape.

Would I have applied for the job if I had known he would be the one interviewing me? I don't think so. I would have run away in the opposite direction.

Getting turned down for that job was the best thing that has ever happened to me—at least it will be if MegaDome turns out to be as profitable as I think it will be.

I'm going to have to do a whole lot more of these concerts, festivals, and extravaganzas if it works out the way I think it will. This could be a real money-making machine.

We make out in the limo on the way back to my apartment. He walks me to the door and we stand there kissing for a long time. He's spending tomorrow at his grandson's Little League game and a family barbecue afterward. Dante needs to sleep tonight and so do I.

Neither of us wants to stop kissing, but we finally tear ourselves away. I go into my apartment and change into my pajamas.

I'm just settling down in bed with my tablet when someone knocks on my apartment door. It's almost midnight.

I open the door and find Rita standing there. That didn't take long at all. She pushes past me to enter my apartment without waiting for me to invite her.

"You've been awfully busy lately, haven't you?" she demands from the middle of the living room.

I slam the door behind me. "Yes, I have. Do you have a problem with that?"

"He's Dante Helme, Emberlynn!" she blares and then cups her hands around her mouth just in case I didn't hear her the first time. "Dante Helme!"

"I know who he is, Rita. I didn't get involved with him without knowing who he is."

She jolts. "Involved! You're *involved* with him?!"

"Yes, I am. Do you have a problem with that?"

"Oh! I don't know!" She pretends to look around. "He's only like thirty years older than you are! He's a grandfather, you know."

"Yes, I know. Is that your only objection because, if it is...."

"He's Dante Helm, Emberlynn!!" she roars. "He's only like one of the richest men in New York! He's a member of The Billionaires' Club! Oh, what am I saying? He's one of the officers in The Billionaires' Club! He's one of its founding members, for Christ's sake!"

"I know all that, Rita! What exactly is your problem with me going out with him? He's a great guy."

"He's old enough to be your father!"

"So what?! He's kind and generous and experienced and steady and supportive. He's caring and protective and considerate. How could you possibly object to me going out with someone like that just because he's older?"

She stares at me with her mouth open and then jerks her head from side to side while she swipes her hand away. "I am not talking to you until you come to your senses."

She walks out of the apartment as abruptly as she walked into it. I heave a deep sigh and go over there to lock all the doors. That was the first blow—the first shoe to drop. Who will be next?

I'm sure the press will have a field day when they find out the great Dante Helme is dating a woman so much younger than himself. Then again, he's been dating women younger than himself for a long time.

He hasn't dated them seriously. The press and the public are used to him hooking up with random floozies here and there, enjoying himself with them for as long as it lasts, and moving on just as fast.

It almost seems inevitable that all the single men in The Billionaires' Club would do the same thing. Giovanni does it all the time. Lane Prince used to do it all the time, too, before he got married.

The only difference is that he's the same age as the girls he hooks up with. The girls are the same. The only difference is Dante's age.

A lot of the single men in the club don't hook up with anyone ever. I can't remember ever seeing a report about Jackson Metcalf hooking up with anyone ever. Niko Holloway never did, either—not before he married Melody Gottlieb.

That was the big scandal—that he got married after spending so many years alone. Jackson will probably never get married. He's a monk—and he isn't the only one.

All the men in The Billionaires' Club seem to fall to one of the two extremes. They're either whores who sleep with a different girl every night or they keep their noses to the grindstone and don't look sideways at anything else no matter how much it throws itself at them.

Dante doesn't fall to either extreme. He isn't a monk and he isn't a player. He's just a healthy man with a normal desire for female company. It isn't his fault that he can't find someone his own age who shares his lifestyle.

I don't share his lifestyle, but I just might wind up starting to if this concert thing gets off the ground. I don't know how I would ever have a relationship with anyone if I'm really going to do this, but that's a question for another day.

I barely think about the confrontation with Rita. My best friend says she won't talk to me until I stop seeing Dante. Is that what my life is coming to—that I have to choose between my friends and family on one side and going out with him on the other?

She isn't my friend if she could turn against me over a little thing like this. I could understand that she was surprised to see me and Dante holding hands at the restaurant. That's no reason for her to bump me as a friend. Am I not worth anything more than that?

She has nothing to say against the relationship except that he's Dante Helme and he's older than I am. He's right. That's really just a confirmation that the relationship is good. She can't say anything bad about it.

I curl up in bed. I don't want to look at my tablet anyway. I already have all those numbers and everything in my head. I don't need to stare at a screen to see it all in front of my eyes.

This is my life now. I guess this is what I am now. I'm a business-woman.

Dante was the first to see it—or he was the first to encourage me to cultivate this new potential in myself.

Would Rita turn against me for planning this concert festival? Would she turn her back on me because I want to grow and become something more?

If she could turn her back on me for something as small as going out with Dante, what's to stop her from turning her back on me for something else—something even more important?

Chapter 15: Dante

Lucas claps me on the shoulder and then straightens the jacket around my shoulder. He grins at me. "Are you ready to go out there and start holding court with all your adoring admirers?"

I sneer at him. "Please. It isn't like that at all."

"Of course it is. They all love you."

I try to make a face, but the noise on the convention floor distracts us.

Lucas tugs his sleeves down. He doesn't want me to know it, but he's getting as excited by this as I am. "I guess we better go out there."

"Wait, son," I tell him. "I want to tell you something."

"Don't make this a father-son moment where you tell me how proud you are of me."

"It isn't that." I take a deep breath. "I'm seeing someone. It's serious. I think....I think she might be the one."

His eyebrows fly up. "Really? That's great. I'm happy for you."

"I just....I just don't want you to freak when you find out."

"Why would I freak? The whole family has been encouraging you to get with someone. You just aren't the easiest guy to shop for, you know? I'm glad you finally found someone who fits with you."

I nod more to myself than to him. I'm more nervous about telling him that I'm seeing someone than about going to this convention.

He claps me on the shoulder again, but he's already looking out there onto the floor. Me going out with someone isn't a big deal to him—not like it is to me.

He says, "I can't wait to meet her," and walks past me onto the convention floor.

I follow him. I can't wait around anymore feeling nervous on Emberlynn's behalf. She'll sink or swim at this convention. Her business idea and this whole concert festival project will sink or swim at this convention.

I see a bunch of the other Billionaires' Club members mingling in the crowd. They talk to everyone, hear a million pitches, and get a bunch of new ideas.

Some of them walk around with paper notepads and pens writing things down or entering ideas and new contacts into their phones.

I cross the convention floor and stop a dozen yards away from where Emberlynn stands talking to Jackson, Judah, Giovanni, Niko, and Melody. Lane is already on his way over there.

I've been telling my friends at the club about Emberlynn, but she and I have an agreement that we won't tell anyone we're involved in a relationship—not yet. They know I'm mentoring her. That's all.

I don't go over there or get involved. This one is all on her. She smiles effortlessly and talks to all of them about the MegaDome Experience, her preparations, and who else is already lining up to invest in her.

MegaDome is skyrocketing as never before, but she doesn't come to me for approval anymore. She doesn't express any doubts. She just handles it.

I have to admire her standing over there talking to some of the richest, most powerful, most influential people in New York. She wears a tailored business suit and winds her hair into a twist on the back of her head. She really looks the part.

It works on the other billionaires. They know exactly who and what they're dealing with when they talk to her. They recognize one of their own and they don't hesitate.

She moves to one side to show her tablet to Giovanni. She keeps all her documentation on that tablet. She shows him a few things and then picks up the glossy printed prospectus from the convention table behind her.

She turns a few pages showing promotional material from the bands she has booked to play Madison Square Gardens, the merch she's getting produced—literally everything.

She's been working harder on this than she's ever worked on anything in her life—and that shows, too. The prospectus includes huge lists of acts, booths, events, displays—everything an investor could want.

She and Giovanni stand there talking for a minute before Judah interrupts. The whole group starts talking. I couldn't be prouder of her, but I can't stay around and watch.

I wander off to another part of the convention and wind up talking to some of my other friends and associates. I don't really want to be here. I just want to talk to Emberlynn. I have to wait for that.

I find her at the lunch break. "How is it going?"

"Great!" Her cheeks flush. "I got a bunch of interested potential investors. They want to send me contracts and everything."

"That's great. You were killing it out there."

She flashes me an excited smile. "I'm proud of myself. This is really going to work."

"Of course it is. It can't possibly not work with the way you're stepping up and kicking ass."

She leans in and kisses me. "I want to celebrate tonight! We should go out."

I pull her to a stop before she rushes off. "Baby.....listen to me." I tug her hand so she turns around and faces me. "I want to introduce you to my family."

She stops dead in her tracks and her jaw drops. "You do? Are you sure?"

"I've never been more sure of anything. What do you say? The only question is whether you're sure."

She bursts into another grin. "Okay. That sounds fun. I want to meet them all—and I'll be able to see you in your native habitat. It will be like a sociological experiment or field mission or whatever you call it ."

I can't take it as a joke. "We get together every Sunday afternoon. You can come over then. We'll be having a barbecue, so it will be a relaxed setting with no pressure or anything like that."

She bursts into another smile. "Yay! This will be fun."

I pull her closer toward me. "I want us to get serious. I mean it. I don't want to wait anymore."

She rises on her tiptoes to kiss me and slips her arms around my neck. "I want that, too." She gets a notification on her phone and steps back to answer it. Then she frowns.

"What's wrong?"

"Oh, my God! I just got an offer to sell MegaDome."

"What do you mean—sell it?"

She looks up at me with huge eyes. "Someone wants to buy the company—the whole festival promotion project. They're offering me twenty million for it—which means I would get a payout of five million—just for myself." Her eyes glaze over. "This isn't happening."

"It's great. All your hard work is paying off."

Her head snaps up. "You really think I should do it?! How could I do that?"

I shrug. "Every business is up for sale. This is no different." I nod at her phone. "Who is the offer from?"

"Angelico Entertainment."

I nod. "That's one of Giovanni's offshoots. It's a legitimate offer. You should take it."

"But....this festival is my thing. I put a lot of work into it."

"And now you're getting paid for it. You don't have to work your fingers to the bone over the next two years and give yourself a bunch of grey hair. That will be someone else's problem."

"But you said I should be working for myself. You said I shouldn't farm out the responsibility to someone else."

"You aren't. You built a successful business and now you're selling it."

"But....I mean.....five million dollars! I don't know what I would even do with that kind of money."

"You could put it toward your next venture. You started this concert thing with nothing. Imagine what you could do with five million dollars. You could do a whole tour if you really wanted to."

"I feel like I should put it aside for a rainy day—or at least part of it. I don't want to stake it on another business—not all of it, at least."

"That's easy enough. You could invest—say—a million in getting yourself a nicer apartment—one you own free and clear with no debt. Then you don't have to pay rent on it or a mortgage or anything. Then you could put a million into some other income-generating asset like a real estate investment or some other vehicle that will pay your expenses for you. That leaves you three million to stake on another venture—something that has the potential to make you even more.

That's the way you build over time. You leapfrog from one to the next and upscale each time to something bigger."

She blinks at me in stunned amazement. Then she shuts her eyes and looks away. "I can't think about this right now. I better go back out onto the floor."

"Just think about it. We can talk over dinner tonight."

Chapter 16: Emberlynn

I blunder back to my table at the convention. I put my phone back in my pocket, but I can't stop thinking about this offer. Someone wants me to sell my MegaDome project. They're going to pay me five million dollars so they can take over the project in my place.

I've been throwing my heart and soul into this. I don't want to give it up—but do I just feel that way because I've been working so hard on it?

The project was never about the money for me. It was more of an experiment to see just how far I could push myself. Is it still about that?

I don't even know how to think about this offer. I go through the motions of talking to a bunch of other investors. They use words like, 'million' and 'billion' in conversation all the time. They don't act like it's anything out of the ordinary.

I'm starting to get used to that, too. This project is definitely worth twenty million. It's probably worth a lot more than that.

I could probably get more for it if I really drove a hard bargain—or if I rode the train longer and took the project closer to its fulfillment date.

I already know I'm going to take this offer. That's the thing. I really don't want to give myself an early heart condition dealing with all the stress and late nights of actually pulling off the festival.

Selling the project means I succeeded. I have to convince myself of that. I did it. I launched a successful business and now I'm selling it. That's the successful endpoint of all business.

That's what Dante always tells me. He says the goal of building a business is never to ride it until the wheels fall off. I really need to listen to his advice. He knows so much more about it.

I get a break in the constant traffic past my table. I'm just thinking about going to sit down somewhere when the crowd parts and someone else comes up to me.

I spot the guy from twenty feet away. It's Lucas from the park bench. He looks completely different in an immaculate power suit.

He shoots me the same winning smile and holds out his hand. "Emberlynn, right? I'm Lucas. Remember me?"

"How could I forget? You never called me."

"I was hoping I could call you to tell you that I found someone who wanted an executive assistant. I thought I could somehow buy my way into asking you out if I found you a job." He looks at the table behind me. "I never expected to see you doing *this.*"

"I guess you could say I started working for myself."

"You certainly did." He turns back to face me. "I guess I don't need to find you a job before I ask you out."

"You're too late. I'm in a relationship with someone. Sorry. You missed the boat."

He doesn't stop smiling at all. "That sucks. I would really like to go out with you." He takes a step closer to me. "So who's the guy? Is it serious....because....you know....if it isn't, I could suggest...."

I push him away. "Don't suggest anything, Lucas. You had your chance. It's too late. You should have asked me out when you first got my number. Then maybe I would be getting serious about you instead of him."

"So it is serious." He takes a step back. "Anyway, I didn't come over here to talk to you about that."

"Are you sure—because it looks like you did."

He only smiles. "Actually, I didn't know you were the one doing this concert project when I came over here to talk to you. My firm represents Angelico Entertainment—so if you accept their purchase offer, you'll be dealing with me on the other end."

I study him more closely. "Is that so?"

"Yes, it is so. Do you have any questions about the offer? I would be happy to go over it with you."

"Are you sure I should be talking to you about that—since you represent the other side? Shouldn't I be getting another lawyer of my own?"

He bursts into another grin. He acts like my comments are the most delightful thing he's ever heard. "Yes, you should. Do you have a lawyer?"

"No, but I'll have to get one, won't I?"

"I can recommend someone if you like."

I make a face at him. "You know I can't take your recommendation on that, either. Don't worry. I have advisors I can ask. I'm sure they'll recommend someone."

He beams at me even more brightly. "I'm really glad I'm going to be facing you across the negotiating table. I really hope it works out for you."

I find myself smiling back at him. He's a nice guy and I like talking to him. I just can't let him hit on me when I'm already getting serious about Dante.

"Are you sure you didn't have anything to do with this deal?" I ask.

"I told you I didn't know you were the one behind it—but no, it wasn't me. Giovanni won't stop talking about you—and not just because you're gorgeous, smart, talented, driven, and easy to talk to. He's a sucker for women like that, but he's an even bigger sucker for an entertainment deal like this one. He can't stop raving about this project. He really wants to buy it. I probably shouldn't tell you this, but you could probably get more for it if you just waited until a little closer to the performance date."

"I already know that and I really think you better stop making comments about this deal. You're the enemy, remember?"

He bursts out laughing. "Aw! I'm hurt."

I have to laugh along with him. "Very funny. Goodbye, Lucas. It was nice seeing you again. I'm sure we'll talk again as this deal goes on."

"I'm sure we will." He walks away laughing. I have to stop myself from smiling. Going out with him would have been fun, but that window has closed.

Now I have to pack up my table and get ready to go meet Dante for dinner. I have to talk to him about getting recommendations for a corporate lawyer to handle the sale.

I have a lot of work to do even to sell the project—and I have to keep it running right up until I do sell it. It has to be a viable enterprise when I sell it.

Chapter 17: Dante

I nearly jump out of my skin when my apartment door swings open. Mark and Delia roll in with all their kids. The kids laugh, yell, and run around the apartment while I talk to Mark and Delia about everything.

Aiden, Roxanne, and Lucas all pile into the apartment next. The noise is just escalating to a fevered pitch when Jay and Tracey enter with Todd and Evelyn.

I get lost in the crowd until Lucas comes over and claps me on the shoulder. "So where's your lady? When do we get to meet her?"

"She should be here any second now." I have to rush back to the kitchen to finish all the preparations for the food and everything.

The others go out to the living room and Aiden opens the sliding doors onto the terrace. The kids are too busy playing tag in the living room. None of them seems to be wearing their swimsuits this time.

I carry a tray of burger patties, sausages, and steaks to the barbecue. Aiden, Mark, Jay, and Lucas are all too busy talking, so I put the steaks on to grill while I go back to the kitchen.

I'm just checking the baked beans in the crockpot when someone knocks on the door. I open it and Emberlynn smiles at me across the threshold. "Hi!" she breathes.

"Hi. Come on in." I kiss her and put my arm around her. "I don't know about you, but I'm a nervous wreck."

She laughs. "That makes two of us. So where are these dragons you want me to slay?"

"In there." I nod to the living room and then pull her into the kitchen so no one can see her just yet. "Are you okay with this?"

She smiles up at me. Her eyes glisten and her cheeks flush. "Yeah. I'm ready. It will be fine, I'm sure." She hands me a carton of ice cream. "I wasn't sure what to bring, so I decided to play it safe."

"That will definitely be safe. I'm sure the kids will give it a good home."

She laughs. "Let's get this over with. I don't want to wait any longer."

"Okay. Here goes."

I take her hand and lead her into the living room. Everyone turns around.

I go through the group introducing everyone. They all shake hands with her and tell her it's nice to meet her. I don't see anyone making a big deal about the fact that she's the youngest adult here. No one comments on her age at all.

They talk to her and find out what she does. She starts talking about the MegaDome project and how she's in negotiations to sell it for millions.

Everyone is suitably impressed. I have to go back to the kitchen to carry some more food to the table. Mark goes out to the terrace to turn the steaks. Emberlynn gets deep into conversation with Jay and Tracey.

I'm on my way out to the terrace when I spot Lucas walking out of the living room on his way to the stairs down the hall. His face twists in fury. He better not start having a problem with Emberlynn.

I don't have time to deal with that right now. I do a bunch of other chores and then get pulled into a discussion with Aiden about how Emberlynn and I met and how I've been mentoring her to start her own business enterprise.

Lucas still doesn't come back by the time everyone migrates out to the terrace. Tracey, Delia, and Roxanne talk to Emberlynn about her time with Marianne Talbot. I don't need to worry about Emberlynn, so I go to find Lucas.

I have to search for him. He better not be hiding from me. I finally locate him on one of the apartment's upstairs balconies. He looks off in another direction even though he can hear all the voices down on the terrace from here.

"Son?" I ask. "Is something wrong?"

"Only that you're dating a woman who is young enough to be your daughter." He looks down at the drink in his hand. "You know, I was really happy that you found someone you could spend your time with after all these years...."

"I did find someone I could spend my time with after all these years. Don't tell me her age is your only problem with her because that's not an argument. She's really great. Why don't you at least talk to her? You might find out you like her."

He turns around and fights to control his features. I've never seen him so mad. "I could understand you hooking up with one of them just for a fling. I never thought you would actually take one of them seriously."

I raise my eyebrows. I have to fight my temper under control. "One of them? You're talking about human beings like they're cattle or something. What's the matter with you? She's a sweet girl...."

"There you go," he snaps back. "She's a girl. You don't even take her seriously..."

I lose my temper and barely keep my voice down. I don't want anyone else to hear us. "You have no idea what you're talking about. You have no idea what has been going on between me and Emberlynn. I could have gotten serious with any of the younger women I've dated. You never had a problem with any of them. That's what this is about, isn't it? You don't want me to get serious with anyone. You've been seeing me single all your life and now you can't stand the thought of me actually getting together with someone."

"That isn't it at all!" he fires back. "You're sixty years old! What is she—twenty-three?"

"She's twenty-seven if you really must know—but it's none of your business how old she is! I'm the one dating her—not you! I was alone for fifteen years raising you and your brother and I've been alone for another ten since then. I think I've earned a chance to enjoy myself. You don't get to decide or approve or pass judgment on who I date, who I get serious with, or who I spend my time with! I'm dating her whether you like it or not. Now if you can't go downstairs and at least be polite, then maybe you should leave."

He glares at me. "So you're choosing her over me?"

"You're doing that. Go downstairs and don't let me see you have a problem with her again. She's here as my guest and you're being unacceptably rude. I expect you to behave yourself around her and welcome her. Don't let me hear again that you have any problem with her or you'll be dealing with me."

I storm out on him and go downstairs. Everyone is milling around on the terrace talking. Emberlynn gives me a strange look when I come out fuming like a volcano ready to blow.

She shoots Lucas a look on the side when he comes downstairs a minute later. She goes on talking to everyone else and so does he, but he keeps his distance from her.

Enough people talk to her, engage with her, and welcome her that she doesn't notice him circling every other part of the crowd. I really hope she doesn't realize he's avoiding her.

He was the last person I expected to have a problem with her—or us. I'm going to have to shut this down.

We sit down to eat. He sits on the other end of the table so he's not in danger of having to talk to her. I can see I'm going to have to deal with him again—for the last time.

We usually hang out for most of the day on Sunday, but Emberlynn makes an excuse to leave after lunch. I don't blame her.

I walk her to the door and then slip out into the hall so I can kiss her goodbye without anyone else seeing us.

"That went really well, I thought," I tell her.

She stands back studying me. "What's wrong with Lucas?"

I cringe. "It's nothing. I'll straighten him out."

I don't understand the look she's giving me. "What did he tell you about it?"

"He objects to the age difference. That's all. It's nothing you need to worry about. He'll just have to accept it. That's all."

"What will you do if he doesn't? It isn't like he would stop being your son just because he objected to me. He's the one in your life—not me."

"Don't say that, okay? You're too important to me."

She doesn't stop me from kissing her, but she pulls away too soon.

"Don't let this bother you," I tell her. "It will work out. He'll come around. I'll make certain of it."

She stands back and evaluates me. I don't like the look in her eyes.

"What's wrong?" I ask, "Don't tell me you're having doubts about us."

"I'm not the one having doubts. You are. You're worried that this relationship will come between you and your son—and you're right because it is coming between you and your son."

"No, it isn't. I won't let it."

She pushes me away harder when I try to get close to her. "Listen, Dante. I don't want to be the wedge that drives you two apart, but I really think you need to talk to him."

"I plan to. I already have and I'll do it again."

She shakes her head. "He isn't worried about the age difference. It isn't that. He's jealous."

I freeze. "What?"

"He asked me out, okay? I met him downtown and we started talking. This was weeks ago—maybe even months ago—long before any of this happened. He asked me out and I gave him my number because he said he knew people who might want to hire an executive assistant, but he never called—he says because he was hoping to find someone who could give me a job. Then he hit on me again at the convention. He didn't know I was the person you were mentoring and I didn't know he was your son. I would have shut it down way sooner if I had known. I told him I was seeing someone and that the door was closed. That's why he's upset. This has nothing to do with the age difference." She raises her hand and turns away. "I think I need to step out while you go deal with this. I'll see you around."

She walks off and leaves me stunned. I can't believe it.

My rage erupts as soon as she walks away. Lucas lied to me. He made it out that he was concerned about me dating someone young enough to be his sister—when that isn't the reason at all. He wants Emberlynn for himself.

I storm back into the apartment. I have to control myself so I can blow up at him in private. I won't do it in front of the whole family.

"She's really sweet," Tracey tells me. "I'm happy for you."

"Thanks," I mumble. "I'm thrilled with the whole thing."

She smiles at me. "I can see that. You have every right to be. She's really exceptional."

I make it through the rest of the evening. Everyone else is super supportive of me and Emberlynn. Lucas doesn't say a word—to anyone—not about that. He talks about everything else and avoids any comment on the subject of Emberlynn.

I wait until everyone is getting ready to leave. I hug my grandkids and grandnieces and nephew. I take that moment to tell Lucas to stick around so we can talk afterward.

That's nothing we haven't done a thousand times before. We usually wind up talking about business when the others aren't around to hear.

I finally hug Jay and Tracey and shut the door behind them. Now I'm alone with my son.

"So......" I have to work hard to control my fury. "You and Ember lynn....She told me you asked her out."

He looks away. So it's all true.

"How could you do this?" I hear my voice shaking. "How could you stand there and make it out that you had a problem with her age when you wanted her for yourself the whole time?"

"It wasn't like that."

"What possible objection could you have to me going out with her—apart from that?" My voice starts rising. "How am I supposed to trust you around her when you can't even be honest with me about it?"

"I didn't know who she was, okay?" he fires back. "I didn't know you were going out with her."

"What the hell difference does that make? You could have just played it off and maybe laughed about it and said, 'Hey, small world, huh?' or something stupid like that! You didn't have to get all bent out of shape and make me feel guilty and make her feel uncomfortable about coming here to meet my family because you got egg on your face."

"I don't have egg on my face!" he snaps. "It wasn't like that."

"How was it then, Lucas?!" I demand. "How was it when you stomped out of the room and hid upstairs and wouldn't even look at her or talk to her or shake her hand? Please—tell me how it was when you sat on the other end of the table and you still have not once congratulated me for actually finding someone after all these years when you and your brother have been hounding me to find someone I could actually connect with. I can't wait to hear you explain this. Her coming to meet my family could have been perfectly relaxing and friendly, but no! You're the one who had to make it awkward and hostile—because you wanted her! Just admit it! Just say the words that you asked her out and now you're pissed that she's going out with me instead! Just admit that you made up the whole age thing to cover your tracks and throw the blame back on me!"

"Fine! I asked her out!" he yells back. "Is that what you want to hear—that I met her downtown and I actually thought she might be the one—and now she winds up here with you? Is that what you want to hear—that I might actually be able to build a future with her—and what are you going to give her? Are you going to keep her until she's an old maid and rob her of her future and turn her into a workaholic like you—when she could get with someone who could actually care enough to give her a life? Jesus, Dad! What are you thinking?!"

I stare at him in horror. He did not just say that—about Emberlynn. I've been falling deeper and deeper over her—and now this happens.

I turn away. I can't even stay in the same room with him with those words hanging in the air. I can't deal with him right now, but he must be thinking the same thing.

He doesn't stick around long enough for either of us to say anything. He walks out and slams the door behind him.

Chapter 18: Emberlynn

I lounge on my couch going over a bunch of documents from Lucas for Angelico Entertainment to purchase the rights to the MegaDome concert festival project.

Lucas Helme. That's his name right at the top of the letterhead. He's Dante's younger son—the lawyer. I still can't believe it.

Lucas's legal firm is Novitiate Associates. He's one of four partners in what could possibly be the greatest corporate law firm in New York.

That doesn't matter because Lucas is representing Angelico Entertainment in this deal. I have my own legal team. They aren't as high up the food chain as Novitiate.

My lawyers actually act intimidated about dealing with him, but the deal is still amicable, so it isn't too bad.

I've had two meetings with Giovanni Nowaczyk, the CEO who owns Angelico. He's over-the-top excited about purchasing MegaDome and turning it into an annual thing that will rake in billions. Maybe I should keep it for myself. I'm still not sure.

I would probably just start doing the same thing all over again once I stop working on MegaDome. I can't think of anything better to do and I guess you could say I got bitten by the bug. I don't want to stop.

I navigate around the internet and look at other, nicer apartments I might buy with my five-million-dollar payout. There are a lot of nice apartments available, but I'm still not sure.

Someone knocks on my door right then. It better not be Rita coming back to haunt me. I'm really starting to wonder if I even want to make up with her.

I open the door and find Dante waiting for me outside. His cheek spasms and his voice cracks with painful emotion. "Hi," he murmurs.

"Hi," I reply. "Are you okay?"

"I...I don't know. Do you mind if I come in so we can talk?"

I open the door for him and shut it behind him, but I'm not ready to pick up where we left off. I don't know how I fit into his life when he has so much conflict on his end.

He paces around the room. He doesn't try to get close to me. "So.....I don't really know what to say..." he begins.

"I'm not sure if we should keep seeing each other," I tell him.

He spins around. "When did you decide that? I told you I would take care of Lucas. We have too much going for us...."

"It isn't that. You might not have a problem with the age difference, but I do. I realized after we talked about it that I do want children. I realize I must have already been thinking it when I mentioned it last time. I think I should get with someone my own age that I can build a future with. I'm sorry. I really like you and we have a great connection, but we're in different places in our lives right now. It isn't personal. It just worked out that way."

"What if I was willing?" he asks.

My head shoots up. "What?"

"What if I was willing—to have children and everything? What if I could give you that?"

"But....you can't! You're.....I mean.....you're old."

He shrugs, but he still has a hard time looking at me. "I want to give you the life you want. I want you for myself. I don't want to lose what we have, but I don't want you to sacrifice your life and your future to be with me."

"But that's what I would be doing. You're going to die before me one way or the other. That's what I would be doing. I would be signing up to raise our children alone—at least some of the time. You should know better than anyone what that's like. Is that what you want for me—for you to die and for me to be left to raise our children alone? I can't believe you would actually want that."

He flinches again. "I guess I can't argue with that, but I at least want to try. I don't want that to be the reason things don't work out between us."

I turn away. I don't want to talk about it anymore. If we're going to break up, then I just want to hurry up, get it done, and move on. I have too many other things I want to work on instead.

"At least consider it," he urges. "Don't completely discount the possibility just because of my age. I have a few years left in me. I might even have twenty years left in me."

"So you can be an eighty-year-old father still raising teenagers?" I grimace. "Come on. Let's not fool ourselves."

"Is that really the only reason?" he asks. "Do you have any other objections?"

"Isn't that enough?" I ask. "I don't need any other objection."

He nods. "Okay. Just think about it—because if that's your only objection, then basically what you're saying is that the rest of our relationship is perfect the way it is. It works. We care about each other. We really want to be together and we have everything we need to make it work—so it could work if we just give it a chance."

I shake my head. "I don't know. Every day I spend with you is another day I'm not with someone I could spend my life with."

"Just think about it, okay? Promise me you'll think about it."

"Okay. I'll think about it."

He comes toward me, makes a moment of deep eye contact with me, picks up my hand, and kisses my knuckles before he walks out.

I don't know how to overcome these objections or even if we can overcome them or should overcome them.

I'm not certain in my decision yet. I guess it all comes down to that. I have to keep considering and thinking about it because I'm not certain yet. I can't and won't decide one way or the other until I am certain.

I'm not certain about the MegaDome sale, either. I need to think about that, too. I have a week to decide. I put everything related to the purchase on hold and just concentrate on working on the festival.

I throw myself into it with all my energy. Maybe that's the answer I'm looking for—that I'm so energized about completing this project and only lukewarm about the purchase.

I'm not chomping at the bit to sell this project I've put my heart and soul into. I don't think I'll ever be ready to sell it.

I spend the rest of the day handling one task after another. I don't look sideways at the purchase agreement or answer a single email from Lucas or my own legal team. They can all wait.

I don't want to give them another minute of my time until I know for certain if I'm going through with this sale.

It's interesting that I find it so easy to put the purchase so far out of my mind. It's the last thing on my priority list. I don't want to think about it. I don't want to look for another apartment.

I keep working on MegaDome. It's so much more interesting and energizing.

I finally finish everything I need to do, sit down on the couch, pull my tablet toward me, and run a completely different set of numbers.

I crunch out how much MegaDome stands to earn if I keep it for myself. I already have a pretty clear idea because I know what Giovanni plans to do with the project as soon as he gets his hands on it.

I also crunch out exactly how much money the project stands to earn in profits if I keep doing it every year.

It could turn into one of the biggest, most profitable enterprises on the Eastern Seaboard. It could become the Burning Man of the Eastern Seaboard with people coming from all over the country or even the world to attend.

I could charge a lot more for entry if MegaDome did get that big. Then the profits would be even higher.

The numbers start to make my head spin. This project—this business—it has too much potential. I don't want to sell it. I *won't* sell it. This is my brainchild—my magnum opus. I won't give it up or sell it for a puny five million dollars.

I can't believe I'm actually calling five million dollars, 'puny,' but it is compared to how much it could potentially earn. That's why Giovanni is willing to pay twenty million for it. Twenty million is pocket change compared to what he'll earn back.

That could be me. I could be another member of The Billionaires' Club—but I don't want that.

I put the tablet aside. I have to email the lawyers and tell them. That's all I have to do, but I don't email them yet. I need to sit with this decision and think about it.

Another knock on my door startles me out of my trance. I don't know who it could be.

I stiffen when I find Dante standing there. He holds a piece of paper in his hand.

"Can I help you?" I ask. "I think we already said everything we have to say to each other."

"Not quite. I think you should have this." He hands me the piece of paper.

"What is this?" I ask.

"I got a sperm count done today. I went to the doctors and got it done—just to clear the air between us."

My jaw hits the carpet. "You.....what?"

"I'm still able to father children. We could do this, Emberlynn. You want someone you could spend your life with. Spend it with me. We'll have children. We'll have the family of our dreams. You can do all of that with me. I might die first—or you might die first. Something could happen to you and I would be left to raise our children alone for the second time. Yes, it was hard, and yes, it would be hard to do it again, but I'm willing to risk that because I believe in us. I can face that for the chance to have something real with you." He points to the paper. "Just think about it, okay? I wanted you to have all the relevant information. That's all."

He walks away and leaves me standing there stunned. Now what am I supposed to do?

Chapter 19: Dante

I step into the front office of Novitiate Associates, my son Lucas's law firm. I stop in front of the reception desk.

"Good morning, Mr. Helme," the receptionist Betty greets me. "What can I do for you?"

"I would like to see my son if he isn't too busy—and no, I don't have an appointment. He doesn't know I'm here."

"Okay. Just give me a second." She picks up her phone, taps on it, and holds it to her ear. "Yes, Sir. Your father is here asking to see you if you have some time. Yes, Sir. I'll tell him." She hangs up. "He says you can go right in."

I thank her and head down the hall to Lucas's office. I stop in the doorway. He stands behind the desk straightening out stacks of file folders. His laptop stands open next to his elbow.

He looks up and stiffens when he sees me standing there. "What can I do for you?"

I pace into his office and turn aside. I put my hands on my hips and look around at nothing while I try to decide what to say. "I need to ask you something.....about Emberlynn."

He straightens up and squares his shoulders at me. I know every shade of his facial expression. He can't hide from me how defensive the subject makes him.

"Okay," he counters. "Go ahead and ask."

I can't look at him. "Would you....would you pursue things with her.....if I stepped aside?"

"I don't know. I guess that depends."

"What would it depend on?"

He hesitates and looks down at his files before he summons the nerve to reply. "Did you have sex with her?"

"Yeah." I choke on the words. "Yes, I did."

"So where do you stand with her now?" he asks. "Did you two break up—because of me? I never intended that."

"No, it wasn't because of you at all." I can't even turn around to face him. "It was everything you said—and more. She wants children. She wants a life and a future with someone her own age—someone she can grow old with—and that's never going to be me. I went to the doctor and got a sperm count done. I asked her to build a life with me. I just want to give her the life she dreams of even if it's with someone else. She should have that with you if she can't have it with me. I know you would be good for her. You obviously have a connection with her. You should pursue it."

He remains silent for way too long. I can't even look at my own son. That's what my life is coming to.

He comes up behind me and lowers his voice. "I'm sorry. I can see that you really care about her."

I try to shrug. "It doesn't matter because it's over. She already made up her mind and she won't change it."

He puts his hand on my shoulder and squeezes. "I'm sorry I wasn't as truthful as I should have been about where I stood with her. You were right about that being wrong of me. I should have just told the truth. I would only be happy for you if it worked out between you two.

I wouldn't want to step in as long as there was any chance between y ou."

"There isn't." I feel my throat starting to tighten.

"MegaDome will be at another convention over the weekend," he tells me. "We'll all be there and so will Giovanni and some of the other investors. We might be able to turn things around then."

I only shrug. I didn't realize before that this would hit me so hard. She really does mean that much to me. She's the only one I want. I'm not ready to let it go.

"Don't give up hope yet," he tells me. "Things could change."

"I don't see how. You should step in."

He falls into another silence before he says, "All right. I will."

I can only nod. Good. He needs someone like her and she needs someone like him. They're actually perfect for each other. I don't know why I didn't see it before.

I regret now that I slept with her. I shouldn't have. I should have seen that she would be better for him than for me.

I didn't think anything would come of it when I hooked up with her the first time. Now it's too late.

I turn around, but I can't make eye contact with him. "I guess I better get out of here."

He says, "I'll see you soon."

I hustle out of the office and drive to my own building. I have a lot of work to do to get ready for the convention, but MegaDome keeps intruding in different ways. I can't ignore it.

Emberlynn is always there—right in front of my face. She'll always be there in front of my face if she gets together with Lucas. She would become my daughter-in-law and the mother of my grandchildren. Am I really ready to deal with that?

I'm not now, but I would just have to get used to it. Time would smooth over all the bumps and hiccups. We would both get used to it eventually. It would become normal.

We might have to go through an awkward transition while the rest of the family gets used to the reality that Lucas was getting together with a woman I dated first. That wouldn't be the most pleasant conversation.

They would eventually accept it. The family already accepts and likes Emberlynn. Lucas would tell them the same thing I told her. If he doesn't have a problem with it, they shouldn't, either.

I want to tell her that I approve of her getting together with him. I want to tell her that I won't stand in their way, but I don't want to keep showing up on her doorstep again and again and again. I've been doing that too much as it is these last few days.

I just need to leave her alone and let Lucas work his magic. He's good with women. He'll straighten things out with her and let her know that he's okay with the situation as long as she is.

Chapter 20: Emberlynn

I zip my laptop case shut and put it in a rolling suitcase full of MegaDome promotional material for the latest convention. This convention is really a chance for me to talk to all the current investors. I don't need any new ones.

This convention is also an opportunity for me to explain to Lucas and Giovanni in person that I'm changing my mind about selling MegaDome. I owe Giovanni an explanation at the very least.

I plan to tell him that he's welcome to invest in the project, but that I plan to keep a controlling share of the company as well as creative control. I'm not ready to give it up—and I'm not doing this to drive the price up. MegaDome isn't for sale—not now.

I'm just checking my phone to go downstairs when someone knocks on the door. I don't have time to deal with Dante right now. He better not be coming back to beg me for another chance.

I open the door and my stomach drops. Lucas smiles at me across the threshold. "If it isn't Nighthawk in the flesh," he teases.

I gulp with difficulty. "Um...what are you doing here?"

"I want to talk to you about my father."

"Um.....okay. We broke up. You don't have to worry about me dating him anymore."

"That's what I want to talk to you about."

"And I'm not ready to start going out with anyone else yet. I'm too busy with MegaDome......and I don't think I could see someone so closely related to someone I've already gone out with."

He laughs. He acts genuinely delighted to be talking to me—again. "I'm not here to ask you out, Emberlynn."

"Why are you here, then?"

"I want you to make up with him. I think you two belong together. He loves you very much. I don't know if he ever told you that, but he does. I've never seen him like this with anyone. I think you two belong together and I think you should give him a chance." He raises his hand. "He explained to me about your objections and your desire to build a future with someone your own age. I understand all of that—but I don't think you should give up on the connection between you. I think you would struggle to build that with anyone other than him. He's a good man...."

"I know he is. I never thought he wasn't."

"Are you aware that he loves you—like really loves you? He's deeply, madly, off-the-deep-end in love with you. Did you know that?"

I look away. "I kind of got that feeling, yeah."

"I bet you feel the same way about him, too, don't you?" he asks.

I can't look at him. I wind up turning my back on him. I don't want to think about my feelings for Dante.

Lucas comes into the apartment without asking for permission and stops behind me. He lowers his voice. "What you two have is special. It might be a once-in-a-lifetime love. Don't give up on that. You belong together. He would do anything to give you the life of your dreams—even if it meant walking away and letting you get together

with someone else. He wants you to have everything you've ever wanted. You might search for the rest of forever before you found someone
like that." His voice breaks. "I thought when I met you that you were
the one for me. That's why I got so upset when I saw you with him.
I saw how much you meant to him and I didn't want to believe that
you were the one for him instead—but now I know I could never give
you what he can give you. I could be your husband. I could be the
father of your children, but I could never be him. I could never give
you that thing you have between you. That's special between the two
of you. Don't throw that away. You both deserve to be happy. The
more I see and hear from both of you, the more I realize you should
be getting it from each other. Maybe you can only get it from each
other. I don't know, but at least try. Don't walk away from it—not
when you have so much working in your favor." His voice changes
again. "Anyway, I just wanted to come and say that. You two should
be together. I'm sorry if I made it uncomfortable when you came over
to meet the family. I promise it won't happen again. I...I guess I'll see y
ou at the convention."

He walks out and leaves the door standing open behind me. I have
to fight down overwhelming emotion. How can someone I don't even
know read so clearly what's written in my heart? What I have with
Dante is beyond anything I've ever experienced.

I don't want anyone else. I don't even want someone younger. I
want him.

I love the fact that he's so much older than I am. I love that he's so
much more knowledgeable and experienced than I am. He makes me
feel safe and protected.

Just standing in the same room with Lucas makes me feel the contrast. He's much younger and has a completely different energy and
personality. Lucas isn't as steady, not as grounded, and more volatile.

I have no doubt that Dante would do absolutely anything to give me the life I most want. He would be there every step of the way. He would never let me want for anything.

He would support me and make sure I always had what I needed—even if it meant stepping aside and letting me get together with someone else.

That's what it all comes down to. My wellbeing is his only priority. He'll do what's best for me even if it's not what he personally wants.

I don't want someone else. I want him.

An alarm goes off on my phone just then. It's time to leave.

I wheel my suitcase downstairs and get in a cab to drive uptown to the convention center. I get out of the car and then forget about everything else while I check in with the organizers and set up my table.

I'm just laying out my promotional materials when Giovanni comes up to me all gushing and blushing with pleasure. Lucas comes with him. Lucas gives nothing away. He just acts like Giovanni's lawyer.

Giovanni laughs when I break the news that I don't want to sell MegaDome after all. "I never should have told you my plans, should I?" he teases. "You're going to be laughing all the way to the bank."

I can't help coloring. "You're welcome to come on board as an investor. We would love to have you."

"Oh, don't think you're going to stop me from coming on board in whatever way you'll let me. You don't have to tell me. You want to run the event your own way."

I shrug that away. "I'm not gonna lie. The money might have had something to do with it, too."

He laughs again and holds out his hand to shake mine. "I don't suppose I could convince you to come work for me, could I?"

"Do you mean become your employee and treat you as my boss? You have GOT to be kidding me."

He laughs again and shakes his head. The other investors interrupt us by coming over. We start talking and Lucas slips away.

I get lost in talking to everyone else. I feel myself getting more and more enthusiastic and excited about this as the day wears on. I'm so much more pumped about MegaDome, now that I know it's all mine. I don't have to share it with anyone.

I spot Dante lurking in the background. I see him watching me from afar, but he doesn't get involved, not even to wish me well or to spend time with his friends.

I know he's doing this because he thinks it's what's best for me. He doesn't want to interfere or overcomplicate the process.

I can't help but see his eyes glow with pleasure and pride when he watches me—and something else. He still wants something with me. Maybe Lucas is right and Dante will always want that. Maybe it can't just end because I said it had to.

Dante doesn't look away when some of the younger conference attendees crowd a little too close and get personal with me. Their energy blasts into me from inches away. They want more, too.

I try to turn away and see Lucas looking back and forth between me and Dante. What if? What is there to stop me from making up with Dante after all if that's what we both want? Why hold back?

I get through the rest of the convention, but I leave my table set up. I'm coming back tomorrow to do it all again. MegaDome can't have enough investors.

Actually, it can. I need to tone it down so I don't eat too much into the profits.

I plan to go home to my apartment and crunch some more numbers about how much I'm going to need, what percentage of the profits I can afford to share with investors—and I need to start paying myself a salary.

MegaDome takes all my time nowadays. I don't want to work for the catering service anymore. I have more important things to do—and this investment money is enough to start paying myself and taking on new staff so I don't have to do absolutely everything.

I'm just walking out of the building when I spot Dante in the distance. He stands off to one side tapping on his phone. No one else is around.

I go over to him and wait until he looks up. His face goes through a bunch of different emotions. "Hi," I tell him.

"Hi," he replies. "You looked like you had a good day."

"I did....but it will be even better if you go out to dinner with me. What do you say? Do you have plans for tonight?"

His eyebrows shoot up. "You want to have dinner...with me?"

I smile at him. "I can't think of anyone I would rather have dinner with." I hold out my hand. "What do you say—just you...me....dinner.....?"

He glances around like he's worried someone will bust him—Lucas, maybe. Maybe Dante thinks Lucas will have a problem with me and Dante going out together.

I don't wait. I step forward, take his hand, and tow him toward the exit. "I know a quiet little out-of-the-way Chinese restaurant right around the corner. No one will bother us there."

"What about what you said about....you know...building a future with someone your own age? What happened to that?"

"Don't argue. Just come have dinner with me. It isn't a lifetime commitment."

"I don't know about this......"

I laugh at him. I really like him. I want him.....and I love him. Lucas is right about that. I love Dante and he loves me. We belong together.

Chapter 21: Emberlynn

I pull Dante into the Chinese restaurant and we get a table together. I smile at him until the waiter leaves.

"Are you sure about this?" He keeps glancing around. "You sounded pretty adamant about your position the last time we talked."

"I've been thinking it over. I don't want to waste what we have. I'm willing to give it a try if you are."

"Give it a try?" He grimaces. "You said you wanted children. We wouldn't be giving it a try. We would be going all in. We *would* be making a lifetime commitment."

"Okay. Let's make a lifetime commitment."

His jaw drops. "What happened to you? What made you change your mind so drastically when you were so certain?"

I shrug. I doubt he wants to hear that Lucas was the one who convinced me. "Let's call it a gut instinct. We might never find another connection like the one we have. I'm sure I could find someone my age who would be a good husband and a good father. In fact, I'm certain I could, but he wouldn't be you. I wouldn't have with him what I have with you—because I can only get that from you. I don't want to live without that."

He looks away and gulps. "I don't want to lose what we have, either. What we have is special."

I take his hand and squeeze. "Let's talk about it. How should we proceed?"

"Maybe you should be the one to tell me. You're the one who sounds so certain about it."

I let go of his hand. "You may have heard that I decided not to sell MegaDome after all."

"Yes, I heard. My son is the purchaser's lawyer, remember?"

I grin at him, but I have to stay serious. "Then you know I'm going to be extremely busy over the next few years—and I plan to keep MegaDome going every year after this. It's going to become an annual event like Burning Man."

His eyes fall out of their sockets again. "That's huge."

"That's what made me decide not to sell it. The profits stand to be so much bigger the longer we keep it going—so I'll be hiring staff and telling them what to do so I have a more normal schedule than I have now."

He nods. "That sounds smart. Have you discussed this with your investors?"

"That's pretty much all we talked about today and probably all we'll talk about tomorrow. I'm going to start paying myself a salary so I don't have to work as a server anymore—and I'll be able to get a better apartment."

Now he's the one who leans across the table and takes my hand. "Don't. Move in with me instead."

"Um....what?"

"Move in with me. To hell with it. Let's go all in. You don't have to get another apartment. Come on. I want you with me. I want us to spend every day together. I don't want to wait—as long as you're s ure."

I have to pick up my jaw off the floor and the waiter distracts us just then. I take too long deciding what to order before he leaves us alone with our fried wontons and sweet and sour sauce.

"You don't have to decide right away about moving in with me," he tells me. "Just....you know.....come home with me tonight."

I smile up at him. "Twist my arm."

"I'm not going to do that, but I want you there. I don't want you living on the other side of town."

I have to think about it and then smile at him again. "Okay. I'd like that."

He wilts in relief and squeezes my hand again. "I really missed you. It killed me to think I had to let go of you."

"Yeah, me, too," I breathe. "I guess that's what convinced me—that it was so hard to let go of you when I knew it was right."

He lets go of my hand and picks up his wanton to dunk it in the sauce. "So tell me what's going on with MegaDome."

"Just what I told you. We're talking about hiring in staff to run the day-to-day operations. I'll be the managing and creative director, but all the other lower-level managers and organizers will be responsible for running the actual festival—and I have to start planning for the following year's festival now. I have to start thinking two years in advance so we keep the momentum going. As soon as we wrap the first festival, we'll already be knee-deep in planning the festival for the following year. We won't have any downtime between them—which is why I need to start working a desk job and keeping regular business hours. I'll probably get roped into working more when the festival actually happens, but most of the time, someone else will be doing that. I'll only get called for emergencies."

"How does that feel? How does it feel to let go of the reins even just a little bit?"

"It's a little scary because I've never done any of this before—but at the same time, I've done it all before when I worked for Marianne. I don't worry about letting go of control. I know I'll be doing that. I was more concerned about it when I was considering selling. That didn't feel right. That really did feel like I was doing the wrong thing. Lucas was really great about it. He's such a great guy."

Dante flinches. "We should talk about him."

"What is there to talk about?"

"He's interested in you. You know it. I know it. We all know it. We need to deal with it."

I sneer. "He isn't interested in me, Dante—not anymore."

"What makes you say that?"

"That's between me and him—but he isn't. He approves of me getting back together with you."

He frowns to himself. "Are you sure?"

"Very sure. Why? What makes you think he's still interested?"

"Never mind." The waiter comes with our food. We spend the rest of the evening talking about MegaDome. Then Dante talks about some of his business deals and how Lucas and his buddies at the firm are so involved in every aspect of Dante's business.

I listen to everything and we head out afterward to go back to his place. Curtis picks us up outside the convention center and we stop by my apartment so I can take a few of my things.

"All of this feels so official," I tell Dante after we get back into the car. "I feel like I'm already moving in with you."

"Just so you know I want you at my place all the time. I understand if you aren't ready for that, but I want you there as much as you're comfortable with."

I slip my hand into his. "I hesitate to say we'll see how it goes, but let's just take it slowly. We don't need to jump right into anything."

"Whatever you're comfortable with.....but I'm not getting any younger, you know."

I laugh. "None of us is." Curtis lets us out in front of Dante's building and we ride the elevator up to his penthouse apartment. It opens onto a rooftop terrace with a pool, trees in gravel beds, the barbecue, and a few outdoor living room areas.

The sliding glass doors are shut now, but I can see all of New York spread out from here. I don't know if I'm ready to live here long-term, but I could sure get used to this.

Dante takes my suitcase somewhere. I've never seen any of the bedrooms in this apartment. I've only seen the kitchen, the living room, and the terrace. I'll have to explore the place once I get used to it.

I wander to the windows until Dante comes back. He eases in behind me, wraps his arms around me, and kisses my hair. "I'm so relieved that you're back," he murmurs. "Part of me was missing without you."

I turn around to face him so I can hug him around the neck. "I felt the same way. I don't know why, but this just feels right."

He leans back to look down at me. "So what do you want to do first now that you're here?"

"Don't we both have to sleep tonight? We both have to go back to the convention tomorrow. We can't afford to stay up late."

"Don't be sensible about it. We could have a torrid convention affair and pretend that we're both visiting from out of town and we'll never see each other again after tonight."

I laugh at him. "It sounds like that's what you want."

"I'm living vicariously through you. Why shouldn't we live the fantasy if we can't live it in reality."

"Something tells me that the reality wouldn't be nearly as enjoyable as you make it sound. Torrid affairs never are."

"Oh, come on. Was that first night we spent together after the gala more enjoyable in fantasy than it was in reality."

"No, but that's because it was you," I tell him. "It wouldn't have been nearly so enjoyable if it had been someone I didn't know and would never see again."

"You didn't know me then and you had no way of knowing if you would ever see me again."

"I did know you. I knew you from all the club functions. I knew you were kind and considerate to all the staff. I knew you tried to take care of everything after I spilled all those drinks. I knew you defended me in front of Ross. You didn't have to do any of that—and I had also seen you being caring and considerate to the rest of the staff, too."

"You could have all of that with someone you met at a convention. You could have a wild night and never see him again. You never expected to see me again, did you?"

I grimace. "No, I didn't—and I don't want to go back to that now. I just want to enjoy being with you—just like this."

I sink into kissing him. I don't want to be anywhere else or think about anything else. I just want tonight. I don't want anything to take me away from just being here with him.

I hold onto him for all I'm worth. The feeling of holding onto him and taking shelter in him—it's more than I ever thought I would experience with anyone.

He holds onto me just as hard. He buries his face in my neck and I feel him shaking with the strain. He never thought he would get me back. This is more than he ever dared to hope for—just in case I wasn't sure if he felt the same way about me.

He does. This means everything to both of us. I can't let go of this. I have to take all of this and make the most of it. I won't find this with anyone else.

I lean back to stare into his eyes. His face hovers before me. I know every line and shade of who he is. He holds nothing back.

His eyebrows pinch at the center and he frowns. I hear his voice coming from a long way off. "Emberlynn? What's wrong?"

I freeze in that moment. I can't answer. I feel something break inside me somewhere. I want to tell him that nothing is wrong—but it is. It's very wrong. It's more than wrong.

A lightning bolt of pure, blinding intensity hits me in the head. I feel myself falling. He barely grabs me in time before my knees buckle and I collapse right there on the floor of his living room.

"Emberlynn!" he roars. "Emberlynn—answer me!"

I barely hear him. I can't see or feel anything except that the world is falling apart all around me. It's too late. I'm already falling and everything falls apart around my ears before I black out.

Chapter 22: Dante

I pace back and forth in the hospital corridor outside the Emergency Department. I don't even dare to go in there. I don't want to find out that something is wrong with Emberlynn—not after I really started to fall so madly in love with her.

I can't lose her—not now. I can't go through that again—not when I just got her back.

I can't believe she just collapsed in my arms. This is the worst outcome I can imagine to what should have been one of the happiest nights of my life.

She was going to move in with me. We were actually going to build a life together. I don't know what will happen to me if I lose that now.

I turn at the end of the hall to pace back the other way. Doctors, nurses, medics, and orderlies pass me. None of them stops me to tell me what's going on with Emberlynn. None of them will even look at me. It must be bad.

She's already been in there for three hours with no word. She could be in surgery—or it could be something even so much worse.

I only make it four steps before my sons walk through the doors to approach me from the other end of the hall. Jay is wearing his white lab coat. He's working tonight. Lucas is still wearing the suit he had on at the convention. He looks furious. He better not start blaming me for this.

They stop in front of me. "Have you heard anything yet?" Jay asks.

I shake my head at nothing. "I....I'm not sure I want to hear anything."

"I'll go find out." He heads into the department and leaves me there with Lucas.

"Are you okay?" he asks.

I look down at the floor and shake my head. He crushes my shoulder in a death grip. I should have listened to her when she said he would be okay with us getting back together.

We're still standing there in silence by the time Jay comes back. "She just got out of surgery," he tells us. "They're moving her upstairs to the detox clinic."

"Detox?!" I gasp. "She wasn't on anything!"

"They aren't detoxing her from anything like that. She went septic. She's on a heavy course of IV antibiotics until the infection clears. Come on. We can find out more once we get up there."

I wouldn't be able to go anywhere without my sons helping me. They take me into the elevator and we ride upstairs in silence. I can barely function. Those words strike terror into my heart. *She went septic.*

What happened? I dread hearing the answer.

We get out on an upstairs floor of the hospital and check in at the nurses' station. The nurses direct us to Emberlynn's room.

A bunch of doctors stand around talking outside the door. Jay goes up to them and asks about Emberlynn's condition.

"She had a uterine cyst that ruptured and went septic," one of the doctors tells him. "The cyst was totally asymptomatic until a few seconds before it blew. We had to remove part of her uterus. She won't be able to carry a pregnancy after this, but it's a miracle we were able to save her life at all. It could have been far worse."

Lucas grabs me by the shoulder again, but I barely feel it. My eyes snap to the room where Emberlynn lies asleep on the pillow. She doesn't know yet.

This is going to break her. No one has to tell me. She would have walked away from what could have been the greatest relationship of either of our lives because she wanted children.

She bet her whole future on it—and now she can't have them. This will destroy her.

I want to run away from the news. I started to bet my future on that, too—on building that future with her. Now it's gone.

The doctors drift away and so does Jay. Lucas stays, but I can't look at him. I'm barely aware that he's here. I can't stop staring into the room. What am I going to tell her? How can I face her with this news?

Time comes to a standstill. I'm still standing there by the time she stirs. She turns her head back and forth on the pillow a few times before she opens her eyes and sees me.

I have to go in there. I sit down on the edge of the bed and press her hand between mine. I want to cry just from looking at her face.

"What happened?" she rasps in a scratchy voice. She looks around. "I...I'm in the hospital." She winces when she tries to sit up.

"You collapsed in my apartment, sweetheart." I hear my voice shaking. I struggle my hardest to hold back tears. I have to be here to support her. It's going to be so much worse for her than it is for me. "They say you had a....a cyst....in your uterus. It ruptured and went septic. You....you've been in surgery for almost four hours."

She leans back on the pillow, shuts her eyes, and groans. She turns her head back and forth before she relaxes.

All of a sudden, her eyes snap open and she jolts alert. "Wait a minute." She frowns at me. "I had a cyst....in my uterus.....?"

I nod and swallow hard. Here it comes.

"I'm.....I'm okay, though, right?" She starts talking faster. "I'm gonna be okay, aren't I? I can still have children, can't I?"

"I'm sorry, baby." I blink back tears. "They say you could have died. They had to remove part of your uterus to save your life. I'm so sorry. No one knew the cyst was there. It must have been lying dormant for y ears."

"NO, Dante!!" She screams at me and starts raving. "No, it can't! You can't say that! It has to be okay!" She breaks down crying. "No! It can't be!"

I start to say, "Baby...."

"It can't be!!" She starts bellowing at me loud enough to bring the nurses running. "It can't! You're lying!"

I open my mouth to say something, but she flies completely off the handle and lunges for me. She lashes out with her fists. I barely move my head out of the way in time to stop her from punching my lights out.

She lands on my body instead and starts pounding me all over in a rage. "NO!!" she roars. "NO!! Get away from me!! Don't you dare pretend you're upset about this!! You got exactly what you wanted!! Get away from me! I never want to see you again!!"

The nurses surround her bed to restrain her. Lucas shows up right then to pull me away from her. He backs me out of the room until so many nurses surround her that I can't see Emberlynn anymore.

She keeps raving, yelling curses, obscenities, and insults at me, and telling me she hates me.

I can't think straight. It's all over. I can't even think well enough to decide what to do. Lucas drags me out of the hospital, puts me in his car, and drives me to his apartment. I couldn't stand to go back to my apartment right now—not after this.

He marches me into the elevator, takes me upstairs, and pushes me down on the couch in his living room. I'm too bruised to do anything other than stare into space.

I could have supported her and helped her get through this—except that I need her to support me and help me get through this. I need it as much as she does.

I was going to become a father again. I was going to have a family again. I was going to go through all the sleepless nights, the sicknesses, the skinned knees and broken arms, the school report cards and behavior incidents, the teenage romance dramas, the worry, the stress, the doubts and fears......

None of that will happen now. The rest of my life looks pretty bleak without that. I was doing fine with getting older until this happened.

Now I'm just a sad, lonely, broken old man with nothing but a whole lot more lonely years in front of me. I can't even enjoy the family I already have because I don't have her or the future we might have lived together.

Lucas does something in his kitchen and comes to sit down next to me. He doesn't say anything. He knows better.

I didn't understand before, but I do now. He said he would step in. I thought he meant he would make a move on her and start going out with her himself.

He actually meant he would intervene and encourage her to see me again. That's why she gave me another chance—because of him.

I can't even acknowledge the gift he gave me because it's gone now. She doesn't want to see me again. She hates me for this even though it twists the knife in my guts as much as it does hers.

She gave us another chance only to have it snatched away. I don't resent her for taking out her pain on me. I'm no good to her for anything else. At least she can take it out on someone.

I can't take it out on anyone—except maybe myself. I'm all alone with this feeling. Lucas is the only one who knows and I can't take it out on him.

I never want to get involved with another woman again. I don't want to risk something like this happening.

He was dead right about me fooling around with younger women. I'll never do that again. I don't want to insert myself into their lives, not even for a brief one-night fling.

I shouldn't get involved with them at all. I should just stay by myself if I can't find someone my own age—someone who is past all that child-rearing stuff. All of that is behind me now.

Younger women should get with younger men. Younger women who throw themselves at me or try to cozy up to me—they don't know what they're doing. They're lost and misguided.

It's up to me to be the bigger person and remove myself from their realm of possibility. That's the responsible thing to do—that and to never have anything more to do with Emberlynn ever again.

Chapter 23:
Emberlynn

I come out of my new office building, but I have to stop there to check another notification on my phone. My phone has been pinging off the hook all day with messages from investors and suppliers about all the preparations for the MegaDome festival.

I'm drawing a regular salary now with a staff to handle some of the more basic managerial tasks. I'm working regular hours—except that most of my time outside of work is taken up with communicating with everyone about MegaDome, too.

At least I can walk around now. It's been two weeks since I got out of the hospital and I still get sore if I move the wrong way at the wrong time.

I'm doing rehab to recover from the surgery. I'm so busy with work that I don't have time to think about what this means for the rest of my life. I make sure I stay busy so I don't think about it.

I answer the notification and keep my face glued to the phone on my way down the block. I pay attention only to my phone so I don't see the kids playing at the school across the street.

I just had to set up shop in a building right across the street from an elementary school. Now I see young children every time I go into or out of the building.

I try to block out their voices, but it never works. This whole disaster hangs over my head. I can't get rid of it. It haunts me day and night.

I can never have children the way I wanted to. The future I saw for myself—it all comes crashing down around my ears.

I turn a corner toward my new apartment building. I'm living in a nice, downtown apartment within walking distance of the office. I don't have to ride the subway hardly at all anymore.

I spend a lot of time by myself these days. I go to and from work. I spend the rest of my time in my apartment. I don't want to see anyone who isn't involved in MegaDome.

I don't want to explain to anyone why I'm unhappy or why I feel like I don't have a future anymore. I don't even know what kind of future I would have. Am I just going to become one of those women who lives alone and works themselves to death?

Marianne Talbot was one of those. I don't want to be like her, but I have no reason not to be. I have basically nothing going for me and nothing to live for. MegaDome means nothing to me anymore.

I only keep doing it because I have nothing else to do. It takes my mind off my problems. I would completely fall apart if I didn't do something.

The noise of kids yelling fades the farther I walk down the street, but right then, a little boy sprawls across the pavement in front of me. He can't be more than four years old.

I stop dead in my tracks so I don't trip over him. I look up from my phone in time to see him fall flat on his face with his arms and legs spread wide. I realize too late that he must have bolted away from his parents who are getting out of a car right there at the curb.

The mother is in the act of unbuckling an even younger child from the car seat in the vehicle's back seat. The boy bursts out in loud sobs. He blares extra loudly for all the world to hear.

The father turns away from helping the mother, comes over to pick up the older boy, and dust him off. The father hugs him, kisses him, and checks his hands and knees for scuffs and bruises.

The mother joins them holding the little one on her hip. The younger child is a girl sucking her two middle fingers in her mouth.

The mother hugs, kisses, and pets the boy, too, until he calms down enough for the father to take his hand and lead the boy away into a nearby store. Now nothing stands in the way of me continuing my empty, miserable, hollow existence.

I keep walking and make it around the next corner before it all catches up to me. I lean against the nearest wall, cover my face, and burst into tears.

This keeps happening at random times of the day, especially when I see families or children going about their business.

I fall apart and let all the anguish pour out of me. I can't live like this, but I have to keep living no matter what. I can't face the pain otherwise.

I can't bring myself to leave just yet. I slouch there sobbing my eyes out. It isn't fair that I have to go through this when so many people are raising families and living happy lives.

I can't stand it that women are out there getting pregnant without even trying. They don't even want to get pregnant. They don't want their own children—and here I'm stuck like some kind of zombie who wants children and can't have them. It isn't fair!

I can't keep feeling this way. I can't take it anymore. I have to straighten up, shake it off, and keep going. I can't keep falling apart every minute of the day—which is what I would be doing if I let myself stop.

I walk back to my apartment building, go upstairs, put my microwave dinner in the microwave to heat it up, and sit down on the couch to answer more emails from everyone who wants to talk to me about MegaDome.

None of these people know that my heart isn't in it. They all think I'm as enthusiastic as ever. At least I don't have to court investors anymore. I wouldn't be able to summon the energy to convince them n ow.

The whole project will keep going from now on. Its own momentum will keep it going. A share of the profits from this year's event will fund next year's event and so on. We won't need to keep soliciting investment. We'll already have enough money to run the event.

I eventually go to bed and wake up the next morning to do it all again. I have to go to a meeting in the morning and then get together with the investors for a dinner meeting.

Giovanni is as excitable as ever. He's almost more excited about MegaDome now as an investor as he was when he thought he was going to buy the project.

I realize in the middle of the dinner that I'm the only woman here. Half the men at the table are members of The Billionaires' Club. The younger men are obviously interested in me, but I keep it strictly professional.

I'm going to have to be honest with anyone I get involved with from now on. I'll have to tell whoever it is that I can't have children. I don't want anyone getting interested in me if they think they can get anything else.

I don't even want to get involved with anyone. What's the point?

The dinner meeting is just heating up when the door opens and a couple enters the same restaurant. I stare in frozen horror when I see Lucas Helme walk in with another woman.

She's beautiful with gorgeous wavy dark hair. They're both dressed up. They must be on a date. He pulls out her chair for her and smiles at her when he sits down across from her.

She sits with her back to me. He sits down facing me and spots me watching him. He inclines his head sideways in a curious, questioning expression. I look away and pretend not to see him.

A heavy weight falls into the pit of my stomach. He's moving on—and Dante will move on now that it's over between us. I would be deluding myself to expect anything else.

Of course Lucas wants a family. He's surrounded by families. His brother and cousin both have children. That was his whole reason for objecting to me going out with Dante. Lucas thought he would be the one to give me that. Now he knows he can't.

Seeing them sours the whole evening. I can't wait to get out of the meeting. All the investors wish me well and we plan our next moves before we separate for the evening.

I have a long walk back to my apartment. It's already getting dark, but I don't catch a cab or the subway. I need to walk to clear my head and get Lucas out of my mind. I'm happy that he can move on and look for someone else. I wouldn't want him to do anything else.

Seeing him drives a nail into my coffin, though. No one will ever seek me out for that—not ever again. People will reject me because I can't have children. People will reject me exactly the same way I rejected Dante.

They'll be right to reject me for that alone. They can think I'm the greatest person in the world. I don't expect anyone to sacrifice their future just because I'm a good person or even a great person.

I was right to reject Dante. I made the right decision.

I turn a corner, and like something out of my own thoughts, I spot him down the street.

He's in a completely different part of town—or rather I'm in a completely different part of town. I wouldn't have seen him at all if I hadn't decided to walk home from that dinner meeting.

He doesn't see me. He stands outside a different school. It's almost seven o'clock in the evening, but blazing floodlights blast across the playground. The school families are having some kind of fair or something with stalls, games, and activities.

He stands outside the fence looking in like a hungry ghost who sees what he wants and can never have it. His shoulders slump under the weight of the world. God, he looks so anguished and devastated!

I never thought how it would be for him. I never thought that losing our future together would be as hard for him as it is for me. I never thought about him at all.

I blamed him. I thought he would be happy about it and think he dodged a bullet. Now I know that was just my way of coping with the devastation.

I couldn't have faced his grief. I couldn't have seen my own pain written in his eyes.

I see it now, though. I said I hated him and never wanted to see him again. I told the truth then. I did hate him. I hated him because I knew he felt the same way and I couldn't deal with that.

My own thoughts come back to me. I can't get together with anyone who doesn't already know. I can't get together with anyone who wants children—or who can have children.

He's the only one left—and at the same time, he's the perfect solution to all of this. I can finally feel that someone understands because he does understand.

I walk over to him. He sees me coming and looks away, but he only winds up looking into the school with that haunted, hungry, hopeless stare.

"Hi," I murmur.

He barely looks at me. "Hi."

I don't know what to say. I can't ask if he's okay because he obviously isn't. I can't stand it when anyone asks me if I'm okay. I'll never be okay again—and maybe he can understand that, too.

I slip my hand into his. He doesn't react except to squeeze it. "They look so happy, don't they?" he chokes. "I never knew....while it was happening, you know.....I never thought.....when I lost my wife....when I had to raise the boys on my own....I never knew then that I was experiencing the greatest joy of my life. I thought I was forsaken. I thought I was going through the worst disaster known to man....but really I was so happy....I was beyond happy....and I didn't know.....I didn't see it.....but I see it now......I would give anything to go through that again....."

A tear streaks down his cheek. He won't even look at me. He only has eyes for all those families. The kids run around, yell, throw food at each other, and some of them even get into fights.

Some of the parents lose their cool and get into it with their kids in front of everyone.

Seeing all of this would have made me cry before, but I don't hesitate to look at it and see it all now. I put my arm behind his back and rest my head on his shoulder while we both watch.

He understands. He can be there for me in ways no one else can—and I understand how it is for him. I can be there for him in ways no one else can. We're the only people alive in the world who can give each other this.

He bends down and kisses me on the hair. He rests his cheek on top of my head while we watch and hold hands. I don't have to run away from this feeling anymore because I'm not alone.

"Come home with me," he husks. "I need you and you need me. Don't disappear on me again."

I shut my eyes. I can't see the children through my tears anyway. "All right. I will."

Chapter 24:
Emberlynn

I step across the threshold and enter Dante's penthouse apartment. This is only the third time I've been here. The last was when I collapsed and wound up in the hospital.

I look around and try to quell the overflow of conflicting emotions that comes rushing back. I was going to move into this apartment before all of this happened. Dante and I were going to build a very different future together.

I sit down on the couch and look out at the lights of New York. Coming back here means something completely different. It means we'll somehow be even closer than we could have been when we were planning to start a family together.

He sits down on the couch next to me. He doesn't try to kiss me or even put his arms around me. This connection between us—it goes so much deeper now. It bonds us at a deeper level—a level even deeper than love itself.

"I was never happy about what happened to you," he tells me. "I just want you to know that."

"I know you weren't. I guess....I just needed to blame someone and you were there. I figured, if you were really sincere about wanting that with me, then you would be one of those people who would go looking for it somewhere else." I look away. "Like Lucas."

"I only wanted it because it was you. I never wanted it with anyone else. I wanted to do it because I would have been doing it with you. I would never want to go looking for someone else to do it with."

"I know that now." I turn around and take his hand. "You don't have to explain. I guess enough time has passed that I can think about it clearly—if I'll ever be able to think about it clearly. It will always bother me, but I guess I'll get used to it as the reality sinks in."

He leans all the way back on the couch and gazes at me. "My only regret is that I couldn't be there for you. I wish I could have done something for you—to help you. I know no one could help what was really wrong with you, but I wish I could have."

I face him. "I should have been there for you, too. I was too buried in feeling sorry for myself to think how it would be for you. That was selfish of me. I should have tried to help you. I shouldn't have pushed you away. I'm sorry about that now."

"No," he breathes. "You needed to—and that's okay."

I don't wait to give myself a chance to second-guess. I lean in and kiss him. I don't want to keep away from him anymore. I need him as much as he needs me.

I fall on top of him on the couch and sink into his arms. This is as right now as it was before. He'll always be the right one.

That's why Lucas finds it so easy to move on. He knows in his gut that I'm not the one for him. I wasn't the right one for him even when we all thought I could have children.

Dante folds me in his arms while we kiss. That kiss doesn't erupt into passion. It just keeps going in slow, sensual, loving comfort. We know each other too well. We understand everything about each other.

We both know what will happen when we go get in bed together. We understand each other's bodies and what we need from each other.

This is much more important—just lying here together on the couch, kissing, and feeling each other next to each other.

He's all I need. I don't have to worry about him finding out anything about me or expecting anything from me that I can't give. I don't have to worry about him waking up one morning and deciding he wants kids after all.

I lean back to look into his eyes. My weight resting on top of him feels so right. Why did I think I belonged anywhere else?

He runs his fingers through my hair and smiles up at me, but it's a sad smile. "The guys at the club are all thrilled to be working with you," he tells me. "They can't say enough about you."

I try to look away. "They're all so much more knowledgeable and experienced than I am."

"You'll learn and catch up. You're holding your own with them—and that's saying something. How is it going, anyway? I haven't talked to you in ages."

"It feels like ages, doesn't it? It doesn't feel like it's only been a few weeks."

"Are you still gung-ho about MegaDome? Do you still think about selling it?"

"I'm not gung-ho about anything—at least, I haven't been since I got out of the hospital. I've been going ahead with MegaDome just to take my mind off of everything else."

"What do you think about it now? Do you think you might change your mind about selling it?"

I shrug. "I might. I just don't have anything else to do, so I might as well keep going with it. Everyone seems to see me as the figurehead of this project now. They all expect me to keep going. I don't want to let them down." I stroke his cheeks. "What about you? You're still doing all the same stuff, aren't you?"

"Sure. I'll be doing all of that for as long as it lasts. I don't think I'll ever quit."

"How has your family been—about all of this, you know?"

Now it's his turn to shrug. "Jay and Lucas have been quiet about it. They're the only ones who know. Lucas has been great. He's been really supportive in a quiet, steady way. He doesn't talk about it. Neither of them do, but he's always there. He just takes really good care of me. He doesn't have to talk about it because he understands."

I look away. "He's going out with someone now."

"I know. He has a girlfriend. It looks serious."

I can't look at him. "I'm glad he's happy."

"This whole thing—it made him a lot more serious about finding someone. I think you did that for him. He realized when he met you how much he wanted that. He thought it was you, and when it wasn't, he became all the more determined to find the person who was it."

"Have you met her?"

"Yep. He brought her home last weekend. She's really nice. We all like her and he's obviously serious about her. They both seem equally serious about each other—which is nice to see."

I settle in on the couch with him. Talking about all of this feels good. It's comforting to know all about these people and for them to know about me. I wouldn't hesitate to see any of them again, not even if it was in the context of getting back together with Dante.

He reads my mind. "I meant what I said earlier. I still want you to move in with me—if you want to. That part of it hasn't changed for m e."

"What has changed?" I ask.

"We both know now that we won't be starting a family together. Nothing else has changed for me apart from that. I don't know what might have changed for you, but I still want you here with me. I still want to be with you even if we can't have that."

I sink down and rest my head on his chest. "I don't know who or what I am anymore."

He presses his lips against my hair. "You're exactly the same person you were before. You didn't have children before and you don't have children now. When I met you, you didn't even know if you wanted children. You thought you were too young even to think about it and decide. Now that decision has been made for you. You thought you were going to take Path X. Now you find out you have to take Path Y instead. That's all."

"You make it sound so simple," I murmur.

"It's simple. I didn't say it was easy. I only say that because I'm in the same boat. I thought I was going to take Path X, too. I thought we were going to take that path together. Then I found out I would take Path Y. That decision was made for me. It wasn't my choice. The only question is if we'll take Path Y together or apart. I see no reason to take it apart when we're both going down the same path together."

I shut my eyes to hide in his presence. He always makes me feel better and supports me. He always somehow explains these things in ways I have no problem understanding.

Tears spring to my eyes—not for the first time. I can finally feel the grief of how unfair this all is. He makes a safe place for me to feel it in a way I didn't let myself before.

I don't kick myself for feeling sad and destroyed by circumstances beyond my control. He makes it okay to feel this way.

I don't have to explain anything to him, either, because he understands. He hugs my head deeper into his heart and kisses the top of my head.

I would never have to explain anything to his family, either. It would somehow be so much nicer to be here with Jay and Lucas. I would know that they know and they would know that I know they know.

I want them around me. I need people who understand—people who don't need an explanation. I need these people so much more than I realized. I need their whole family—and now I have it—right here in Dante's arms.

Chapter 25: Dante

Emberlynn shoots me a sidelong glance when she comes into the kitchen and takes a bowl of marinating steaks out of the fridge. "Am I allowed to approach the Sacred Pyre or is that strictly forbidden to women?" she asks.

I laugh. "You can put the steaks on the grill as long as none of the High Priests see you near the Altar of Destiny once they get here."

She laughs, too, and heads out to the terrace to put the steaks on the barbecue. Then she carries out the stack of plates and cutlery I put on the counter for her.

She makes half a dozen trips before she comes back and gets herself a wine cooler out of the fridge. "How much longer on the baked beans?" she asks.

"They'll stay in the crock pot until we sit down to eat." I take a minute to kiss her on the cheek.

This is the first time another person has ever helped me prepare for a family barbecue. I usually do the job alone.

She goes around the apartment straightening up. She's been staying here off and on ever since our relationship restarted two weeks ago. This will be the first time she's stayed for our family get-togethers.

She feels a lot more comfortable with it this time. I'm way more nervous than she is. I haven't told my family that Emberlynn and I are back together.

Lucas knows, but he's the only one. Jay is the only other person who even knows Emberlynn and I split up. The others don't know anything about it and they don't need to.

She's still going back and forth and giving me significant glances when Mark and Delia show up with the kids. They all greet Emberlynn and even hug her.

She falls right into it like she never left. She doesn't let on that she's been in a deep depression for over a month—nor does she let on why. She greets the kids, talks to them, and shows them where the food is out on the terrace. Then she starts talking to Delia.

The same thing happens when Jay and Tracey come with their kids and then Aiden and Roxanne arrive. We all wind up talking the way we usually do.

We're standing around shooting the breeze and enjoying our drinks when Lucas walks in with his girlfriend, Desiree. She's almost as tall as I am with long, sweeping, wavy black hair.

She's a bombshell, but I've never met a sweeter girl anywhere. She has a soft-spoken, very feminine, almost vulnerable personality. She isn't brash and bossy. She never imposes on anyone, but she can hold a conversation like nobody's business.

She works as a paralegal in another law firm. That's how Lucas knows her. She isn't ambitious to become something more than what she is, but she commands a vast store of knowledge about just about every subject.

She has an understated way of saying what she knows and contributing to the conversation without stepping on anyone's toes, not even when she corrects them about something she knows that they got wrong.

She has a way of almost making a person glad when she corrects them because she's so damn nice about it. I can definitely see why Lucas likes her. Hell, everyone likes her.

Lucas hugs Emberlynn, kisses her on the cheek, and introduces her to Desiree. Emberlynn and Desiree start talking.

They magnetize to each other and talk to almost no one else all afternoon. Dang. They sure have a lot to say to each other. They look like they're making friends.

Emberlynn talks to everyone about everything. They all act like she never left. She might have been here the whole time.

I get lost in the crowd except for the times when she comes into the kitchen to help me serve the food. I steal kisses from her, but we're both too busy with everything else. We hardly spend any time together for the whole afternoon and into the evening.

I don't see her having a hard time being around the kids—not until later when she goes to the bathroom and doesn't come back. I go looking for her and find her sobbing in the bedroom.

I sit down next to her on the bed and put my arm around her while she bawls into her hands. "I'm sorry!" she howls. "I shouldn't be spoiling this for you."

"Never mind about me," I murmur. "You've been holding it together all this time."

"I don't want to end every one of these barbecues in tears! It isn't fair—and the kids are so sweet and beautiful—and Desiree is so nice!"

"Yeah," I croak. "She is."

"Why?!" she howls. "Why did this have to happen?"

I can only hold her and kiss her. I don't have any answers.

"I'm sorry," she finally sobs. "I'll get used to it in time."

I kiss the side of her head. "It's okay if you don't."

She breaks down again. I give her a box of tissues and she eventually goes into the bathroom to wash her face.

Lucas gives me a strange look when I come downstairs alone. He pretends nothing is wrong and looks in the other direction when Emberlynn returns.

She sits down on the couches with us and goes back to talking to everyone about everything. They're all over-the-top impressed with the whole MegaDome project.

The first advertisements are coming out and tickets are going on sale. Lucas and Desiree already have tickets.

"I want to go to MegaDome," Todd tells Jay.

"You can't," Jay replies. "It's happening over a week in the middle of the school year. You would have to miss school."

"So? What's wrong with that?" Todd turns to Emberlynn. "Kids can go, right?"

She raises her hands. "Kids can go as long as they have their parents' permission and the parents are there to keep an eye on the kids. You better talk to your dad about this. I'm staying out of it."

Todd turns around and narrows his eyes at Jay. Jay narrows his eyes right back. The rest of us laugh.

Emberlynn blends right in with the rest of the family until the end of the evening when everyone leaves. No one bats an eyelash that she stays in the apartment with me afterward.

We lounge on the couch talking and sipping the last of our wine before we eventually go crash in the bedroom. I don't even want to call it my bedroom anymore.

I use my fingertip to comb her hair back behind her ear. "When are you gonna move in with me for real?" I finally ask.

Her head snaps around. "Huh?"

"You heard me. Don't play dumb. You know we've been moving in that direction for a long time. Come on. Sell your apartment and move in here. Don't keep stringing me along."

She looks away.

"What's wrong?" I ask. "Isn't that what we've been working toward all this time?"

"I guess so," she mumbles.

"Did you think we weren't?"

"No, I knew we were. I just....I don't know what's bothering me except that I have all the same problems I did before. I don't want to saddle you with a basket case."

"You aren't. Why do you even tell yourself that?"

"Well, it just happened again today, didn't it? I can't keep making this a problem for you."

"You aren't making it a problem for me, sweetheart." I smack my lips in annoyance. "You aren't a basket case. If you are, then I am and I'm saddling you with the same thing. It isn't a problem. It's just your life now. It's the reality and it doesn't matter if you cry about it every damn day for the next twenty years."

"Well, maybe it's a problem for me," she mumbles.

"Fine. It's a problem for you. Then the only question is....is it going to be a problem for you living over there or is it going to be a problem for you living here?"

She turns around to stare at me. "You really don't have a problem with it?"

"Will you listen to yourself? This is the whole reason we belong together. This is the whole reason I want you to move in with me—because we're both going through the same thing and I need that around me right now. I know it's that way for you. Why do you hide from it when you know this is what you need?"

She sinks down on top of me and rests her head on my chest. "Fine. I'll do it."

I laugh at her. "Don't do me any favors."

She doesn't take the joke. "If you're sure you want that."

"Why wouldn't I want you? Why would you think that?"

She doesn't answer. We just lie here in the silence. She'll move in with me and that will be the end of it.

In a little while, we'll go upstairs to our bedroom—both of ours. She'll move around the apartment like she owns it—because she already does. She's the woman of my heart. I never want her to leave.

I want her to make this apartment her home. She'll make it my home as soon as she does that. I never want her to leave—and she never will as long as we both just keep loving each other enough.

Chapter 26:
Emberlynn

D ante and I ride up the elevator to my new apartment—my soon-to-be-ex apartment. I've only been living here for a few months and I'm already putting it back on the market. I don't care. It doesn't mean as much to me as moving in with Dante.

I've already packed up everything I want to keep. The moving company will come and bring everything over to his place in the next week.

I go into the bedroom and pack my suitcase with everything I want to use before that happens. I pack up my work clothes, shoes, accessories, bathroom products, makeup, hair appliances, and a few other things from the bedroom. That's all I need.

I take down the MegaDome posters I've stuck to the walls, roll them up, and pack up the promotional leaflets, prospectuses, and other printed materials. I might need them, but I can't think of how right now.

Everything else I use on a daily basis is already over there at his apartment—the apartment that's about to become our apartment. I already basically live there. Not much will really change between us.

I set my suitcase on its wheels. Dante calls Curtis to come get us and we head downstairs for the last time. I don't even look back at the apartment. It means nothing to me compared to the future I'm going to have with him.

Becoming part of his family fulfills something I lost when I found out I couldn't have children of my own. I don't know why I think that, but I can still have a family—just in a different way.

Dante and I stop on the sidewalk outside to wait for Curtis to show up. The limo pulls around the corner and heads down the block coming closer to us. Dante and I take a few steps closer to the curb so we'll be ready to get into the car as soon as Curtis pulls in.

The limo makes it to within fifty feet of us before another car angles into the empty space where the limo would have parked. The car is a dinky four-seater passenger car with a man and a woman in the front seat and two little boys in car seats in the back.

The mother is just twisting around in her seat to do something to the younger boy. The father puts the car in *Park* and switches off the motor.

At that moment, a heavy-duty flatbed construction truck pulls into the space behind them coming way too fast. Curtis doesn't get a chance to steer the limo out of the main traffic lane.

The truck loses control, hits the passenger car from behind, and squashes it in a split second. The car's front end hits the vehicle in front of it, which is another hefty delivery van.

The impact flattens the car's hatchback rear end and drives the whole engine compartment backward into the driver's compartment.

The force completely demolishes the front half of the car, obliterates the space where the two parents were just sitting, and leaves only the back seat intact.

Metal fragments and broken glass detonate from the car. Dante leaps in front of me, grabs me, yanks me away, and rotates his back to the wreck to protect me from the danger, but it's all over in a second.

Curtis has to rip the limo into the other lane to stay out of the line of fire. He winds up having to drive past the wreck and keep going with the flow of traffic.

He leaves me and Dante standing there staring in stunned disbelief at the catastrophe in front of us. The two little boys scream when the truck hits their car from behind.

Dante recovers first and charges forward trying to do.....something. The driver's compartment doesn't even exist anymore.

The two parents sit there facing forward in silence with their faces and chests flattened against a wall of wreckage right in front of them. No one could have survived that.

The boys stare around them in stunned confusion for a minute and then the older boy starts screaming. He can't be more than three. His noise sets off his two-year-old brother. They both start shrieking in confused terror.

Their voices send a shiver up my spine. I let go of my suitcase, rush over to the car, and open the rear passenger door. "It's okay!" I tell them. "You're going to be okay!"

"MOMMY!!" the older boy howls. "MOMMYYY!!! I WANT MOMMYY!!!"

"Okay, baby!" I start unbuckling his safety harness, but that only sends him into a frenzy. He stretches his arms toward the passenger side of the driver's compartment.

I don't even want to look at the parents. I lift the older boy out of his car seat to pull him out of the car. He thrashes, twists, and tries to stretch toward the driver's compartment to reach his mother.

The littler boy strains against his harness to get out, too. He screeches just as loudly for his mother, but he winds up stretching his arms toward me.

A white-hot knife stabs me in the heart when I see this little cherub holding out his chubby little arms and calling me, *Mommy*. I can't resist him.

I unbuckle him and try to talk to him as encouragingly as I can while I gather him into my arms. I have to use one arm with him while I try to restrain his brother with the other.

I hold one boy in each arm. The younger boy grapples onto me way too tightly and won't let go. Dante comes my rescue and takes the older boy out of my grasp so I can back out of the car.

I'm just straightening up when the Police pull in with their sirens blaring. They surround the car and the Fire Department moves in to try to assess the parents.

I don't see until I stand up that the truck driver is pacing around tearing out fistfuls of his hair and trying to explain all of this to the officers.

Dante and I back off holding one boy each. Both of them are crying too hard to talk or think straight or answer questions about anything. The older boy stops struggling and holds onto Dante. The younger boy crushes my neck in a death grip.

Dante and I back all the way to the building wall behind us. Curtis drives past more than once, but he can't get near us with all the emergency vehicles standing around.

I don't want to leave yet until we find out what's going to happen to the two boys. Holding onto this child and murmuring comforting things to him does something to me.

I don't want to let go of him—not unless I'm going to give him back to his parents or someone who can really take care of him.

That is never going to happen. It becomes more and more obvious with every passing second that the two parents are both dead—as if I didn't already know that.

I find myself looking over at Dante. He knows exactly what he's doing with the little boy in his arms. Dante holds the boy with expert ease. Dante is a master at this. He looks like the boy's father—or maybe grandfather.

Both boys settle into our arms. The boys are more interested in watching all the emergency workers. Neither boy asks for their parents again.

Do these boys even realize what happened? Neither of them is old enough to understand that their parents are dead and not coming back.

The Police and firefighters only try for a few seconds to extricate the parents' bodies. Then the Police stand back and start running the car's license plate number through their system to find out who the parents are.

Dante and I stand off to one side for more than an hour. None of the Police come to tell us what to do with the boys.

"Do the Police even know these boys were in the car?" I ask Dante after a while.

"Let's find out." He steps forward to approach one of the Police officers. I go with him to see what's what.

"Excuse me," Dante begins. "These little boys were in the back seat of the car—in those car seats. We took them out right after the wreck to keep them safe. What should we do with them now?"

The officer turns around and then looks back and forth between us and the two car seats. This seems to be the first time anyone has realized that there should have been two kids in the back of the car.

The officer directs us to go stand where we were before so we're out of the way. Then he gets on his shoulder radio and calls in the matter to someone else. I don't see what the situation is or how they'll resolve this.

A few different people come over to talk to the officer. Two of these other people are plain-clothes cops wearing badges in their jacket pockets.

It takes a long time and a lot of discussion before one of the plain-clothes officers comes to talk to me and Dante. "We can't locate any other relative to come and take the children, so just wait a little longer and we'll call CPS to take them to a foster placement."

"Don't do that!" I blurt out. "We'll take them home. The boys can stay with us until you find a relative to take them."

Dante spins around and stares at me, but he doesn't argue. The officer frowns at me. "I don't know about that. I could let you take the boys home, but it would only be for a few hours until the social worker comes to make a decision in the case. We have temporary placements for situations like this....."

"We could be a temporary placement," I tell him. "Just let us take the boys until the social worker makes a decision. Please. Don't send them to foster care."

The detective raises his eyebrows. "All right. Just wait here."

He goes back to the uniformed officer. They hold another conference and then they get some of the firefighters involved.

The firefighters unbuckle the boys' car seats from the back and bring them over to us.

Dante gives the officers our names and phone numbers, transfers the older boy to his other arm, takes out his phone, and holds a conversation with Curtis about when, where, and how to pick us up.

Curtis has to park on the next block south of us. Dante and I pick up a car seat each and walk down there to meet the limo.

Dante doesn't tell me I'm crazy for offering to take these boys home. I catch him making eye contact with me on the way, but he doesn't argue.

Dante directs Curtis to go back to the crash site to get my suitcase while Dante and I figure out how to buckle the car seats into the back of the limo.

We put the boys inside the passenger compartment so they can climb around on the seats and check everything out while we work.

Curtis comes back long before we finish. He pushes Dante aside. "Get out of the way, Mr. Helme. I have three kids. I'll do it."

Dante and I move over to the other seat. We have our hands full managing the two boys. They're all over the place.

Then it takes another act of God to buckle the two kids back into their seats for the ride to Dante's penthouse. "I'm hungry," the older boy complains.

"We have food there," Dante tells him. "You can eat as much as you want."

"Do you have carrots?" the boy asks.

The younger boy chimes in and says, "Cawwots."

Dante smiles at both of them. "Yes, I have carrots. What else do you like to eat?"

"Crackers," the older boy announces. "And yogurt."

Dante nods. "You're in luck. I have both of those."

"What about pickles?" the boy asks.

"I don't have pickles, but I can get them from the grocery store."

The boy makes a face. "I hate pickles."

Dante laughs. "Then you're in luck again because I don't have any. What's your name?"

"Benny," the boy replies.

"I'm Dante and this is Emberlynn." Dante holds out his hand and Benny shakes it. "What's your brother's name?"

"Charlie," Benny replies.

Dante checks his watch. "It's almost lunchtime anyway. We'll eat lunch when we get to my house."

"Where's your house?" Benny demands.

Dante points through the limo's front window. "It's right over there. You'll see."

Chapter 27: Emberlynn

The limo pulls up in front of the Dante's apartment building. It takes an age to unbuckle the kids and take out the car seats. Curtis gives us curious looks when he sets the car seats and my suitcase on the curb. "Will there be anything else, Mr. Helme?" he asks.

"That's all, Curtis. Thanks a million for your help. You're a life-saver."

Curtis raises his eyebrows at the two boys. "This is why people keep the car seats inside their cars all the time."

He gets into the limo and drives away into the traffic. "Sage advice," I remark. "Something tells me we won't be driving these kids around in your Miata."

"Don't get attached to these boys. I'm sure CPS will send them back to their relatives as soon as the social workers find someone to take them."

I cringe. I don't want to think about anyone taking these children away from me. I want to keep them even though I know I can't.

Dante gives instructions to the doorman of his building. The guy carries the car seats inside and puts them by the front desk while we get into the elevator with the boys.

We ride upstairs to Dante's penthouse. The boys immediately start running and climbing all over the place, playing with all the stuff on Dante's shelves, and exploring everything.

Dante's grandnieces and nephews have all grown up here, so the apartment is already childproof. He goes to the kitchen and makes a bunch of plates of snacks for the kids to eat.

He lays out baby carrots, crackers, slices of cheese, fruit, and a few rolled tubes of sandwich meat on plates. He carries that, some individual yogurt cups, spoons, and a bottle of carbonated lemonade to the living room coffee table.

He doesn't try to make it formal. He calls the boys over and lets them stand at the coffee table while they stuff themselves.

"You're an expert at this, aren't you?" I ask.

He makes a face. "This is Rule #1. Never overcomplicate anything. Keep everything as simple as you possibly can. Raising kids is hard enough as it is. Don't make it any harder by adding unnecessary friction or trying to impose any outside expectations. Just keep them fed, comfortable, and entertained. That's the whole job right there in a nutshell."

I smile at him, but I have to pay attention to cleaning up all the crumbs, dropped food, spilled lemonade, and then Charlie starts choking on his lunch meat. He sprays chewed-up meat fragments all over the table, the carpet, and all over Dante.

We both work to clean up the mess. The boys eat as much as they want before they lose interest and go back to playing around. Charlie tries to climb onto the couch, falls on his seat, and starts crying for no reason. He didn't get hurt.

I go over to pick him up, but he only blares louder. "He's tired!" Dante yells over the noise. "He's probably in the habit of taking a nap about this time of day."

"What do I do?" I ask.

"Sit down over there and cradle him in your arms so he goes to sleep."

I sit down on the couch. I've never cradled a child in my arms before. It feels strange, but it also floods me with painful emotion. I look down at Charlie's little two-year-old face. He's gorgeous and beyond precious.

He calms down when he stares back up into my eyes. He nuzzles into my arms and relaxes. It still takes a long time before he shuts his eyes and falls asleep.

Dante puts the food in the kitchen and comes back with a book. He hands it to me. I look down at the title. It's, *Mike Mulligan and His Steam Shovel.*

"Come over here to the couch and sit down next to Emberlynn, Benny," Dante tells the boy. "She's going to read you a story."

Benny comes right over, climbs up next to me, and leans against my side. I have to balance Charlie's sleeping body while I turn the pages. I start reading the book out loud.

I only make it a few pages before Benny passes out, too. He slumps against the side of my arm. I can't move under the weight of both boys.

My heart overflows with so much emotion feeling them lean on me. I want to keep doing this. I want to keep taking care of them. I don't want to let go—ever.

Dante is right. I can't get attached to them. CPS will come and take these boys away from me. I have to be ready for that. I even have to be ready for CPS to send the boys into foster care.

Dante and I aren't even really living together yet. I was just getting ready to move in here this morning.

We did have all those discussions about having children together. Why couldn't we give these boys the home they need—if they don't already have some relatives somewhere to do it for them?

I sit there in blissful silence for fifteen minutes before I get a call on my phone. I have to unwedge my arm from under Charlie's sleeping body so I can pull out my phone.

Then I have to bend all the way over so I can put the phone to my ear, but his body gets in the way. I finally give it up and switch the phone to speaker. The screen says, *Rita*.

"Hello?" I ask.

"Hi, sweetie," Rita tells me. "We just got the call from the Police that you and Dante took those boys away from the crash scene."

"Yeah, we did." I hesitate. This is a very different conversation than the one I had with her last time. "Are you the social worker handling the case?"

"I wasn't going to be, but I asked my supervisor to let me take it because I know you. Let me guess. You're at Dante's place right now, aren't you?"

"Um.....yeah. I am. Is that going to be a problem?"

"Not at all. I have his address. I'm on my way over there right now. I'll see you in a few minutes."

She hangs up. I don't know what to expect from her, but she talks in a much calmer, almost soothing voice now. Maybe she's finally coming to her senses and accepts that Dante and I are a couple now.

The boys don't wake up. They're still lying against me, sound asleep, by the time Rita shows up. She has to talk to the doorman who calls Dante on the phone for permission to enter the building.

He opens the door before she gets here. He greets her at the threshold and holds out his hand. She shakes it perfectly politely. She shows no sign that she ever had a problem with our relationship.

He shows her into the living room and she sits do on the couch opposite me. She bursts into a grin when she sees me. "Wait!" She laughs, takes out her phone, and snaps a picture of me. "This is priceless!"

I try to change the subject. "What's going to happen to them? Did you find someone to take them?"

"No, we can't locate any relatives. Their maternal grandmother lives in Omaha, but she's in an aged care facility, so she isn't an option. The paternal grandfather is also alive, but he's serving a life sentence in Riker's Island, so he's out, too. It looks like we need a foster placement for these two and all our current caregivers are booked up." She takes a notebook out of her purse. "The officer at the scene said you would be interested in taking the boys."

I glance up at Dante and he glances down at me. I don't want to say we're interested when we haven't even had a conversation about it.

Dante breaks eye contact first "Yes, we are interested in taking the boys," he tells Rita. "My grandkids come over here all the time, so the place is already set up for kids."

"We have a few extra safety rules for children who are in state care." Rita hands him a pamphlet. "I can assign you as an emergency placement. Then we need to do an assessment on the living arrangements. Both boys need to have their own rooms—and all kitchen knives and any other potential weapons should be locked away at all times. The information is all in that pamphlet. Once you complete the assessment and a Police background check, we can assign you as a temporary placement."

"How long does that last?" I hear my voice shaking. Is this really happening?

She shrugs. "It can last indefinitely unless and until the court rules that a child or children be placed in permanent state care. That usually happens in cases of severe abuse or neglect where the parents are deemed unfit. We don't usually get children who come into the system because their primary caregivers have died and there are no other relatives to take over."

"So....what happens then?" I ask. "Do the kids just stay temporary forever?"

"It just depends on the case. In some cases, the kids stay in one home for their entire childhoods on a temporary placement and the foster caregivers raise the kids as their own without any permanent designation."

"How likely is that to happen?" Dante asks. "What could cause you to take the children to another placement?"

She makes a face. "At this point, it's really up to the caregiver. We have way too few caregivers for the number of children who need to go into the system. If the child is happy there and the caregiver is on board, the child stays. We have nowhere else to move the child most of the time. We don't have a choice."

"So...." I hesitate to say anything to draw her attention back to me. "So you'll give us this placement?"

She glances down at the two sleeping boys. "It looks like they've already made that decision for me. I don't see anything here that doesn't give me the utmost confidence in your care and attention." She stands up. "I'll send you over the documentation, but consider yourselves an emergency placement for now until we finish your assessment. Have a good evening—oh, and by the way, these assessments usually go better if a couple is married."

She leaves me stunned. That was way easier than I thought it would be. I thought we would have to jump through a whole bunch of hoops—and I thought she would make it so much more complicated because Dante is part of this.

Silence falls over the apartment, but it doesn't last. Benny wakes up first and attacks any food left on the plates in front of him. His noise wakes up Charlie.

He starts crying and sits on my lap looking around for something. His two-year-old brain recognizes that something is missing and something else is very out of place and not what he remembers. He just doesn't remember what it is that's out of place.

Benny doesn't seem to notice at all. He goes over to the sliding glass doors, gets his grubby fingerprints all over the glass, and starts yelling when he sees the pool.

Benny gets Charlie's attention and Charlie scrambles out of my lap to go see for himself. Dante opens the doors to the terrace.

The pool doesn't have a fence around it, so Dante and I go out there to supervise the boys. Benny decides he wants to go swimming, but neither of the boys has a swimsuit.

Dante finally takes off all their clothes and lets them go in naked. He goes inside for a few minutes, comes back in his trunks, and goes in with them to help Charlie.

The boys splash and scream in the shallow end. Charlie stays near the steps while Dante sits on the bottom of the pool within arm's reach to rescue Charlie if he needs it.

I stand off to one side watching and laughing. This is so sweet.

The boys eventually get out and decide they want to go back inside. Dante and I dry the boys off, get them dressed, and I watch them while Dante goes to change.

He finds a bunch of crayons and a stack of paper, puts everything on the living room coffee table, and sits down next to me on the couch. He puts his arm around me while we talk to the boys about what they're drawing.

"It's happening," he murmurs in my ear during a lull in the conversation.

"What is?" I ask.

"From your lips to God's ears. You said you wanted children. You said you wanted a family. Now you got one." His eyes lock on mine with heart-stopping power. "You're a natural at this. You're going to be a wonderful mother."

Those words send an electric thrill through me. It's happening. We have a family.

He turns to gaze down at the boys. "You heard what your friend said. These boys are probably too young to remember their parents' death. They'll grow up with us and we'll raise them as our own. We're the only family they'll ever have."

I rest my head against his shoulder and put my arms around him. "You're a wonderful father, too."

He laughs. "I have a lot of experience, but I made plenty of mistakes when I first started out. You're going to need to learn to be patient with yourself more than them. Giving them the benefit of the doubt is easy. All you have to do is love them enough. It's a lot harder not to expect perfection from yourself."

"I'm so glad I'm doing this with you. I wouldn't want to do it with anyone else."

He kisses me on the top of the head. "Everything is working out for the best. You'll see."

Silence falls over the living room except for the gentle scratching of crayons on paper.

"You heard what she said," he goes on. "We have to get married."

I laugh at him. "Is that supposed to be some kind of threat?"

He leans back and stares deep into my eyes. "Marry me. I love you. I want us to be a real family."

I dive in and kiss him. "Yes. I'll marry you."

We both turn to look at the boys. "They're beautiful," I breathe. "They're such a blessing."

"So are you," Dante replies. "You're the best thing that has ever happened to me."

Epilogue: Dante

I stick my head in the fridge and have to squat all the way down to lift a big watermelon off the lowest shelf. I'm just balancing it in my arms when something hits me from the side. I almost drop the watermelon before I correct.

"Dad!!" Benny yells in my ear. "Mommy said they need a towel by the pool!"

"They have towels by the pool. Everyone brought their own."

"Not that kind of towel! She needs a kitchen towel. Charlie dropped his ice cream and it went all over the pavement."

"Oh, okay. Go get one from the drawer."

"Which drawer?" He looks toward the stove.

"Not there, silly. The kitchen towels are under the tin foil...over there."

I wave to the other side of the kitchen by the sink. He pulls open the drawer, grabs a towel, and races away. Now I can lift the watermelon without getting steamrolled by overexcited kids.

I carry the watermelon out to the picnic table. Emberlynn has to keep going back and forth between helping Tracey, Delia, and Roxanne set the table and Benny and Charlie playing in the shallow end of the pool.

Emberlynn gets halfway through setting up a cutting board and knife for me to put the watermelon on. Then she has to stop what she's doing to go straighten out Todd who is splashing water in the younger boys' faces. Tracey goes over there to play bad cop, too.

Aiden, Mark, Lucas, and Desiree sit at the table helping themselves to the food while Jay works the barbecue. I start cutting up the watermelon before Benny charges over soaking wet and dripping water everywhere.

He tries to sit down on the bench next to Lucas and drenches the side of Lucas's shirt and pants. "Hey! Watch it, little bro!" Lucas exclaims. "Dry off before you cause a flood!"

Benny barely notices until Emberlynn sweeps in with a swimming towel, wraps it around the boy, and tries to dry off Lucas's clothes. "I'm so sorry, Lucas," she tells him. "I feed him. I swear it."

Lucas laughs. "Don't worry about it. I needed a bath anyway."

She wraps up Benny in the towel, sits next to Lucas, and puts Benny down on the bench on her other side. Charlie shows up a second later and wants to climb into her lap.

"Go get that towel over there first." She points to one of the deck chairs.

He drags it through the puddles, brings it over to her, and she wraps him in it before she sets him on her lap. Both boys start shoveling the food into their mouths.

"Don't you boys know you aren't supposed to eat fifteen minutes after you swim?" Aiden asks.

"That's fifteen minutes *before* you swim," Delia corrects from the other end of the table and then bellows across the pool. "Leave your sister alone, Todd, or you'll have to get out of the pool."

Conversation restarts around the table. Tracey comes over and sits down on Benny's other side. Mark's kids line up on the other side and Delia starts serving them.

Benny and Charlie have been living with me and Emberlynn for six months. They blend in with the crowd now. No one even notices them anymore.

Life is starting to smooth out for me and Emberlynn. We're settling into a routine.

She works from home so she can field calls and make decisions about MegaDome while she takes care of the boys. We're looking at kindergartens where Benny can start school next year.

Jay comes over from the barbecue to get himself the fixings for his burger. "I got those medical records you asked for on the boys' grandparents," he tells Emberlynn.

"Great!" she exclaims. "Did you find anything?"

"The boys' mother had Type 1 diabetes. She was on daily insulin injections from the time she was four years old, so that's something we'll need to keep an eye on. The paternal grandfather's medical records from the prison say he had a tumor removed from his lung last year, but that's from a history of chronic smoking. I'm still waiting on the boys' father's medical records."

"Thanks, Jay," she exclaims. "I really appreciate it."

"Sure thing. I'll send everything over to you so you can take a look."

"Is that allowed?" I ask. "Aren't people's medical records supposed to be confidential?"

"Foster caregivers are allowed access to medical records relevant to the children in their care. You have to find out all the relevant information so you can give the boys adequate care. The parents are both deceased, so it isn't really an issue and the paternal grandfather gave consent to share his records with you for the boys' sake."

"Aw! That was nice of him," Emberlynn remarks.

"The prison doctor I spoke to had a conversation with him about it," Jay goes on. "The grandfather expressed a desire to write letters to the boys if you're okay with that."

"I think it's great," she exclaims. "They need as much contact as possible with their biological family."

"You might not want them to have as much contact as possible with him," Mark points out. "He's a convicted felon serving a life sentence."

"He's still the boys' grandfather," Emberlynn tells him. "I'm sure the boys can decide for themselves when they get older how much contact they have with him. It isn't like they'll be driving up to Riker's every weekend to visit him. He can't have that much influence on them."

"I'm glad we don't have to worry about that," Lucas remarks.

Emberlynn turns to frown at him. "What do you mean?"

"I mean Desiree and I won't have to worry about our child's grandfather being a bad influence on them." He bursts into a grin. "She's pregnant—and we're getting married."

Cheers, whistles, and applause break out around the table. Everyone grabs him and Desiree, hugs them, and Jay and Mark shake Lucas. All the women crowd around Desiree talking a mile a minute.

We form two different huddles—the women on one side and the men on the other. The kids look on trying to figure out what the big deal is.

The women start bombarding Desiree with questions about all her wedding plans. I take a piece of watermelon and join the men's group. "So what's the plan?" I ask Lucas. "The wedding plan, I mean?"

"We want to get married before she gets too big." He turns to me. "Actually, we were hoping we could do it here—just our family and hers. What do you say?"

"Of course. This is wonderful. I'm so proud of you."

"I had a great role model—and I still do." He claps me on the shoulder and we both turn to look at our families mingling together. All their voices blend into one tide of happiness surrounding all of us.

The kids finish eating and go inside to play with their games and toys. The next generation just keeps expanding, growing, and bringing this world to life. Now a new family is about to come into our world and bring all the energy and fulfillment full circle.

That's the beauty of living this life a second time around. I know now how special it is and I get to appreciate it while it's happening. I wouldn't miss this for the world.

End of Book 5.

Keep Reading

The Billionaires' Club Series: Book 6: Broken Idol

Giovanni Nowaczyk is the biggest player in The Billionaires' Club. His money attracts all the girls he could ever want—and he doesn't shy away from enjoying as many of themas he can get. He can have a different girl every night—so why shouldn't he?

The greatest disaster of his life strikes when a catastrophic car accident leaves him wheelchair-bound and paralyzed from the waist down.

No girl will look at him when he enters a room. He has to give up on the idea of getting a girl ever again for the rest of his life.

Mila Knapp is the only person who sees him for the person on the inside—and Giovanni doesn't like what she sees. The clash of personalities will send them down a dark road of self-discovery to confront their worst fears and overcome impossible odds to build a new life they can both be proud of.

The disasters don't stop once Giovanni and Mila see the light at the end of the tunnel. Their love will be tested by the ultimate challenge of potentially losing everything they hold dear.

You can find it at your favorite book retailer.

Get All of AE Moran's Free Books

S ign Up Once—Get all A.E. Moran's free books including brand new releases

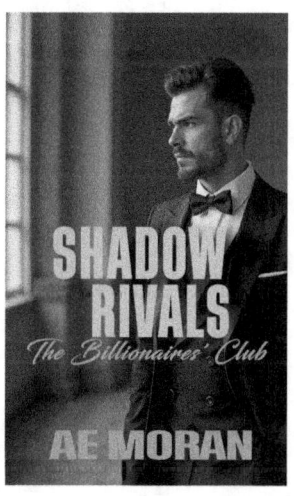

Holden Seager is hot, magnetic, and filthy, stinking, obscenely rich. He commands a room the minute he walks in the door. So what happens when meets another shark as powerful, as charismatic, and as successful as he is—not to mention ten years younger? When these two meet across the negotiating table, one of them will walk away the undisputed winner. The other will walk away with nothing.

Or so it seems.

Unless they're best friends.

When the business deal of a lifetime falls flat on its face and neither of these titans knows how to bring it back to life, this might be the opportunity Dayna Turner has been waiting for.

There's just one problem. She works as an assistant to one of these powerful men....and she's in love with the other. It's a recipe for disaster and heartbreak—unless Dayna can pull off an even bigger coup that will leave them all richer, happier, and more closely connected than ever. The alternative is the destruction of everything all three of them have worked so hard to build.

Sign up at www.authoraemoran.com to read it for free.

About AE Moran

A.E Moran is the contemporary romance pen name for Theo Mann.

I write 70 books per year—and yes, before you ask, all these books are my original creative work. Nothing written under my name is AI-generated or ghostwritten because I write better than AI and any ghostwriter out there.

People don't read fiction for entertainment or to escape from reality. People read fiction to see their humanity reflected in another person's character and story.

This is my promise to you. When you read my books, you'll see your own humanity reflected in the characters and stories. I take this commitment to my readers very seriously. My books are an intimate form of communication between us. I would never disrespect my readers by turning that over to a machine or another writer. This is my bond between me and you as my reader.

I write 20,000 words per day as my daily work output. If anyone with a public platform would like to challenge me to prove this in a controlled environment, feel free to contact me on this website's contact page.

I worked as a professional ghostwriter for fifteen years. Now I'm going for the Guinness World Record by writing 700 books over the next ten years and 1400 books over the next twenty years, all originally written by me. See my website for the full book list.

I'm also the author of *Proof for the Existence of God* and the *Crimes Against Fiction* blog. You can find all my nonfiction work at www.crimes-against-fiction.com.

If you have a story idea, or if you would like me to explore a series in more depth, or if you'd like me to explore a character by writing a spinoff series about that character or world, leave me a message on my website's contact page. I answer all reader emails, so ask me anything, tell me what you liked and didn't like, and let me know where you'd like your favorite series to go. I would love to hear your ideas and find out what you'd like to read next.

You can find out more at www.theomann.com or at www.authoraemoran.com.

Also by AE Moran (so far)